A WOLF'S PROMISE

THE KINCAID WEREWOLVES #4

L.E. WILSON

EVERBLOOD
PUBLISHING

ALSO BY L.E. WILSON

Deathless Night Series (The Vampires)

A Vampire Bewitched

A Vampire's Vengeance

A Vampire Possessed

A Vampire Betrayed

A Vampire's Submission

A Vampire's Choice

The Kincaid Werewolves (The Werewolves)

Lone Wolf's Claim

A Wolf's Honor

The Alpha's Redemption

A Wolf's Promise

A Wolf's Treasure

The Alpha's Surrender

The Sergones Coven (Dragon Shifters & Vampires)

Fire of the Dreki

Blood of the Master

le@lewilsonauthor.com

Paperback Edition ISBN: 978-1-945499-22-7
Publication Date: June 13, 2019
Cover Design: Wicked Smart Designs

CHAPTER 1

Muzzle tinged red with the fresh blood of a deer, Lucian rounded a curve of the mountain trail. Evergreen trees towered over him, obscuring the moonlight and filling the air with the strong, damp smell of pine. He padded over to the ledge and looked down. Beneath him, a few modest properties snuggled up to the base of the mountain. Far enough away from each other to afford privacy, but close enough to feel secure in having a neighbor within walking distance. The scent of their fires tickled his nose, and every now and then he saw a human pass in front of one of the lit windows of the houses, oblivious of the creatures in the dark watching them from above.

He envied them sometimes. Humans. They had no fucking idea of the dangers happening all around them or the things they shared their world with...or the creatures that protected them from some of those dangers. There were times Lucian wished he could throw the unknown into their faces, just to bathe in their shock. To see their happy little lives get tossed upside down.

But what purpose would that serve? It wouldn't make anything better for him or his kind. If anything, it would make it worse. Because humans, as history has proven time and time again, don't acclimate well to anything considered "other". They either enslave things that are different from them, or hunt them for trophies to hang over their mantles. No doubt they would do the same to things like him, in their "appreciation" for that protection.

With one last look, he decided it was time to go home. The others were waiting for him, and despite his frustration with them, his sense of duty to the pack weighed heavily on his shoulders.

An emotion he recognized well, but couldn't name, tore its way through his chest as he started to turn away from the cozy scene below. But before he could leave, movement in the trees far below caught his eye. Sitting back on his haunches, Lucian tilted his head and watched through the mist floating midway down the mountain as a girl burst from the woods directly below him and ran across the stretch of cleared land toward a small, white house in the distance.

Two figures emerged a few steps behind her, their excited grunts and hisses reaching his sensitive ears over the girl's heavy breathing. Her pursuers ran with an awkward lope, their bodies twitching so hard one of them stumbled and fell. Lurching to its feet, it quickly caught up to its friend again.

An olc.

No, worse.

Soul suckers.

Baring his teeth, Lucian threw himself over the side of the drop off. The way was steep, and he half ran, half skidded down the mountain, landing hard on his haunches when he reached the bottom. He used the momentum to spring after the things chasing the girl, covering half the distance between them with one leap. The smell of rotten meat soured the cold air as he neared, confirming he'd been right. These two were Dark Fae, overripe with dark magic and crazed with the hunger for humans. If he didn't catch them before they reached the girl, they'd suck out her soul and leave her corpse for the crows.

Lucian pushed forward, weighing his options. There was no way he could take them both down from behind in enough time for her to get to the house. And even if she managed to make it, it wouldn't matter. Once they knew where she was, a few walls never stopped these things. Though a little sheetrock and paint did wonders to hide the scent of humans if the crazed ones didn't know they were in there.

Unfortunately, these two would know exactly where she was hiding.

Making a decision, Lucian lowered his head and lengthened his stride. When he reached the *an olc*, he pushed hard off the ground with his back legs, leaping over their heads and landing directly behind the girl. He caught a whiff of honey flowers right before he spun around to face them. The scent lingered in his nose, sweetening the air with a memory that danced right on the edge of his thoughts, but he had no time to nail it down.

Disgust rolled through him as Lucian faced off with the two Faeries, their sour scent overpowering everything else, and the wisp of memory blew away with the stench. He bared his teeth and growled in warning to distract them from the hunt. It was enough to give the things pause in the face of this new threat. In their efforts to slow their momentum, they stumbled over their own feet and each other so as not to run into him, and Lucian took full advantage of their surprise.

With a vicious snarl, he clamped his jaws around the bony thigh of the one closest to him and tossed it out of the way before going after the second. The diversion gave him time to remove its head before the first one launched itself back into the fight, wrapping its stinking limbs around Lucian from behind and sinking its teeth into his shoulder.

With a grunt of pain, Lucian leaped off the ground and flipped over in midair, landing on his back with the thing beneath him. The impact jarred them both, and Lucian let out a yelp of pain as he felt its teeth tearing through the skin and muscle of his shoulder.

Scrambling to his feet, Lucian bared his teeth. Wasting no time, he pounced on top of it before it could get up, tearing into putrid muscle and petrified bone, ripping it apart with his powerful jaws. When it stopped moving, he stood watch over the remains, just to be sure, before he released his jaws and spit out the shoulder and a piece of an arm, gagging in disgust.

Tremors of adrenaline ruffled his fur as he caught his

breath, ears pricked for any indication there were more of these fuckers, or worse, that the human neighbors had noticed the ruckus. He heard nothing but his own breathing, and that of the girl.

She stood about twenty feet away, hair dripping with the rain that had begun to fall during the fight and which was quickly turning into a right downpour. She blinked against the wind and rain as she stared at him, her stunned expression frozen in a mixture of disbelief and horror. Her scent blew to him on the cold breeze, and Lucian stilled. It filled his nose, teasing the back of his throat as he inhaled the smell of honey flowers deep into his lungs, knowing he should flee, but unable to force his paws to move.

Finally, after long minutes that felt more like days, she pushed her hair out of her face and wiped her eyes, her movements jerky and hesitant. From this distance he could see the freckles spattered across her cheeks, white with terror, and the shock of blue-green color in her eyes. Lucian realized too late, as usual, what he had done. There would be no explaining away what she'd just witnessed, especially when he would have to shift back to do it.

Moments like these were the times he envied the bloodsuckers their ability to fuck with the memories of humans.

Angry with himself for jumping into the fire without thinking of how it would burn, and unsure what to do now that he had, Lucian began to pace back and forth with nervous energy. His mind spun with different ways he could fix this mess he'd caused as he kept one eye on the girl, constantly gauging her reaction. The heavy rain soaked his fur, but he barely felt it. All he could think was he needed to leave. Run away. Eventually the details of her memory would fade, and her tales of a giant man/wolf would seem less and less believable, even to her own ears.

The headless bodies, however, would be a wee bit harder to ignore.

"I know what you are."

Lucian tilted his head at the first sound of her voice. Though it was a bit on the shaky side, the dulcet tones rippled over his fur, easy as a warm summer breeze. Gooseflesh rose on his skin as her words sank in. But, she couldn't know what he was. Not truly. It wasn't possible unless she was "other", like him. And if that were true, she wouldn't have been running from the soul suckers. Or living here.

No. She was human.

His steps picked up speed. Back and forth. Back and forth. In his gut, the instinct to escape waged a fierce battle with the inexplicable need to remain near this human girl.

Her voice gained strength. "And I know you can understand what I'm saying. So, thank you. For helping me." She paused. Looked to the side before bringing her gaze back to him. The directness of it made him uncomfortable, and utterly aware of her. He must look a monster to her. Not truly a wolf. Not truly a man.

But, if she was frightened of him, she certainly hid it well. "If you promise not to eat me, I can look at that shoulder wound for you."

Even in this form, his nostrils flared with her scent and his body hardened with eagerness. An image of the two of them lying skin to skin with his face buried between her legs pushed out every other rational thought. Lucian shook his head hard, scattering the fantasy and focusing back on the here and now.

Could it be possible this human really knew about his kind? It wasn't completely unheard of, but it was very rare. Few humans who did were allowed to remain living, for the safety of his species and others like him.

Without Lucian being aware, his pacing brought him closer. He caught another whiff of that enticing scent again, stronger now. Flowers dripping with honey. Bog stars. The white flowers that grow in the north. Flowers and warm female.

The scent made his mouth water. He could see now that she was not as young as he'd first thought, but a woman full grown into her thirties, at least, though the unassuming way she carried herself—and the freckles— had thrown him off at first. Her arms were wrapped around her waist against the cold, pushing her breasts up out of the low neckline of her short-sleeved shirt. A woman's full hips filled out the loose pants she was wearing. They were too long for her legs and too tight around her hips and belly, and the dark plaid design reminded him of a pair of his own PJ's. Perhaps she had a male in that house, waiting for her, and those were his pants she was wearing. But if so, why was she out here alone, running around at night in her—or his—sleeping clothes?

"My name is Keelin," she said. "Keelin Doran."

Though her voice still trembled just a bit, she stood her ground as he came closer yet. Lucian's steps gradually slowed until he came to a stop directly in front of her. His nose was at a level with her breasts, and the urge to take that final step forward and bury it in that soft sweet warmth was nearly irresistible.

"Please." Her eyes, so big in her wee face, begged him. "Let me help you. And maybe, in return, you can tell me what the hell to do with this—" She glanced around at the body parts lying behind him. "—*mess* in my lawn."

Tell me what the hell to do... His hackles rose. The only way he would be able to *tell* her anything was if he wasn't a wolf. Och. She wasn't telling tales. She knew exactly what he was. He glanced over at the bloody arm lying nearest him. Lucian had nearly forgotten about the soul suckers, so caught up had he been with the woman. Aye. The lass was right. He couldn't just leave bodies strewn about her lawn. Catching her eyes with his, he lowered his head once and raised it again, hoping she would understand.

With a nervous shift of her eyes, she nodded back. "Good. Come on inside."

She turned to lead the way into her house, head down to shelter her face from the rain and arms wrapped tight around her middle against the cold. Her hair, longer than he'd first assumed, nearly reached her waist. And as he followed the length of it down her back, it was hard to get up the will to follow her, so much did he appreciate the view of her walking away. But, eventually, he managed to put one paw in front of the other and padded along behind her, eyes on her sweet arse, barely resisting the urge to take a bite from the mounds of flesh. Not to hurt her. Only hard enough to get her attention.

A growl of a different sort rumbled through his chest at the thought.

Keelin glanced back over her shoulder, eyes alight with worry. Lucian ground his jaws together and looked away. She followed the direction of his stare for a moment, brow furrowed as she tried to see what he was growling at through the rain, then she turned and climbed the few stairs up onto her porch. At the back door, she turned to him. "Let me grab some towels before you come in, if you don't mind."

Lucian paused just outside the door, rain pouring down on his head and back. With a small, apologetic smile she rushed into the house, closing the glass door but leaving the storm door open.

While she was gone, he took the opportunity to change back. The process went quickly, now that he was calm, though no less painfully. He'd find out pretty damn quick if she'd meant what she'd said when she'd told him she knew what he was.

Keelin returned, her eyes lowered to watch her footing and her arms full of towels. When she looked up, one hand reaching for the door handle, she let out a startled scream to find him crouching naked in the rain with his hands covering his nether regions.

Lucian stood without thinking, both hands up to shush her.

Keelin's eyes dropped to his manly parts. Her mouth fell open, then snapped shut again with an audible click as she quickly looked up at his face.

Yanking the door open, he grabbed a towel from her arms, shaking it out before wrapping it around his hips to hide his nudity. He scowled at her forced expression, schooled into a careful mask despite the flush in her cheeks. "Dinna be so surprised. It's cold an' raining. Ye'd be much more impressed if it was the middle o' summer." With the towel wrapped securely around his waist, he looked up in time to catch her averting her eyes. "I'm sorry. I dinna mean tae sound so crabbit, or tae startle ye. I just thought it would be better tae get the shiftin' done when ye weren't around tae witness it. It can make anyone a wee bit squeamish, even a brave lass like yerself."

The lass in question took a step back, putting some space between them, but otherwise gave no indication that she knew who he was or where he'd come from.

Perhaps he'd misunderstood? "Ye did say ye ken what I am. Is that no' true?"

She took another step back. Lucian followed, only enough to close the door to prying eyes, but didn't get any closer. The lass was feart. That much was obvious. Despite her brave words just a short time ago. "Ye said yer name was Keelin. Keelin Doran, ya? Tis a fine Irish name for a bonnie lass." Lucian grimaced. He was blethering on like an idiot, but thought if he just kept talking, eventually she would snap out of whatever had a hold of her and they could get on with things. "My name is Lucian. Lucian Kincaid. I was no' actually born a 'Kincaid', but I took the name when I was adopted into my pack. My family. I was verra grateful—"

"You're a werewolf. A shifter."

So, the lass hadn't lost her wits after all. "Aye. That I am."

CHAPTER 2

Keelin knew who this wolf was the moment she came out from the spare room and saw his red hair and handsome face, and she was now very glad she hadn't told him more than her name.

This was Lucian. One of Cedric Kincaid's pack. After the war his hatred of the Fae had become notorious. As had his fighting skills. Which she'd just seen firsthand. He'd taken out those two sick Fae with hardly any effort at all. They'd had no chance against him.

However, if what she'd been told about him was true, she couldn't blame him for his feelings. She'd heard rumors that the *an olc*, the Dark Fae, had killed his family. And after everything that had happened to her lately, she wasn't very fond of that particular tribe of Fae herself. As a matter of fact, she strove to live a life as anti-Faerie as possible, for as long as she could.

And now, standing in her quaint country kitchen with this particular wolf, her heart fluttered in her chest like a bird captured within her ribcage. Or, maybe an entire flock. Not because his immense size took up most of the room—which it did. Or because of his stunning good looks—although he was certainly a sight. But for reasons she, being who she was, had no right to feel. Keelin's eyes traveled from the top of his red head, down over his muscular shoulders and arms, rippled abs, lean hips, strong hands, and long, powerful legs. Even his feet were attractive, as far as feet went. Yes, this was a male who would send many a female's hearts all a flutter.

And if that's what he looked like shriveled up from the cold…

No. Fear was not the reason Keelin's heart was racing.

His stormy blue-grey eyes narrowed in on her face, lit with intelligence that was way too sharp for her liking. "Ye said something about fixin' up my shoulder, lass? I would appreciate it, if ye were still up tae doin' it. Help it heal faster."

Keelin could've smacked herself in the forehead. Why the hell had she offered to do that? It had been a reflex. Sometimes her soft heart got her into situations better avoided. Like the current situation, for example. "Uh, yes. Yes! I'm sorry. You just caught me by surprise. I hadn't expected you to be…uh." She waved a hand in the air, taking in his state of undress, and overall humanness. Smokin' hot humanness. "Let me go get my first aid kit." She hurried from the room, calling back over her shoulder. "Have a seat. I'll try to find you something to wear, too." Because Lucian Kincaid in nothing but a towel was wreaking havoc on her libido, and she needed to keep her wits about her if she was going to get through this night unscathed.

She returned a short time later with her kit and some clothes she'd grabbed out of the spare bedroom where she'd packed them away. Just a pair of jeans and a plain white T-shirt, but it was something. They'd belonged to someone very dear to her, and as she handed them over, Keelin had a hard time keeping her voice from catching on a burst of emotion. "You're probably a little tall for these, but at least you won't attract undo attention."

He searched her face for a long moment, but all he said was, "Thank ye, Keelin. I hope they won't be missed by the owner."

He ran the syllables together in her name, pronouncing it in a proper Irish accent like her mom always had, unlike Americans, who said each syllable distinctly, making it sound like "keening", only with an "L". She cleared her throat. "No. No, they won't be missed." Taking a breath, she pulled out one of the chairs that surrounded the small, round table in the breakfast nook. "Why don't you sit and I'll look at that bite."

Setting the clothes on the table, Lucian held his towel closed as best he could and sat. He did it out of deference for her, she knew, as shifters were not normally prone to modesty. But though he managed to keep most of himself hidden, it didn't cover the long length of thigh, lightly dusted with dark red hair and thick with muscles that flexed as he moved.

Keelin quickly averted her eyes and focused on the back of his shoulder. The bite was bad, even for a supernatural creature like a werewolf. It looked like the Faerie had bitten near down to the bone and managed to tear some muscle away when he was dislodged. As she got a clean cloth and wet it at the sink, she tried to think of something to say to fill the awkward silence. "So, where did you come from?" Her hands trembled under the running water. She willed them to be still, but her thoughts ran amok. Had he been watching her? For how long? When did they find out she was here? Did they know who she was?

"I was out for a run, and happened tae see ye run out from the trees, those fookers on yer tail."

She came back to the table. He could be lying. "You were down here? Near humans?"

"No' exactly. I was up on the ridge."

His answer distracted her from the way the ends of his red hair curled on his nape. Softness and strength. Her hand paused just above his wound. "On the ridge?"

"Aye."

"And you jumped over?"

"Aye." This last came out on a sigh.

Remembering what she was supposed to be doing, she gently wiped at the blood covering the skin just above his shoulder bone. "You could've been hurt a lot worse than this. Not that I don't appreciate you running to my rescue," she was quick to add. "But it probably wasn't the smartest thing you've ever done."

He flashed her a devastating smile over his good shoulder. It held a hint of malice. Toward her? Or the things he'd killed? "No chance o' that, lass. And yer wrong. I've jumped from places much higher 'n' steeper. Yer wee hill was nothing. Like skiing down the kiddy trail of a mountain." He winked and faced forward again as she dabbed away the blood. She tried to be gentle. Big, strong wolf or not, it had to hurt like a bitch. But to his credit, he didn't so much as flinch.

"This looks like it needs a few stitches if you want it to heal without leaving an ugly scar."

He glanced back at her, brows down low, shadowing his bright eyes. "Can ye handle a few stitches, lass?"

"I don't think I have much of a choice," Keelin muttered. "You'd heal badly before we got to a hospital." The bleeding was already coagulating. If stitches had to be done, they needed to be done now. "Let me go see if I can find a sturdy needle and some thread." She patted him on the uninjured shoulder. His skin was hot. Was that normal? "Be right back. Don't go anywhere."

She hustled back to her own bedroom this time and went directly to the closet where she kept a bag packed for emergencies, and where she had a travel sewing kit stuck into the top outside pocket. Her house was outside of a small town, the mortgage under a different name so it would be easy for her to up and leave when the time came. And though she loved living in the mountains of the cold northwest corner of the U.S., she knew that time would come. Someday. And when it did, she would be ready. And she wouldn't shed a tear for the life she had to leave behind. As a matter of fact, it would be a relief, if bittersweet.

Keelin looked around her cozy bedroom. She wasn't quite ready to leave this life yet, but now that she had been found, it seemed that time was upon her. Taking a deep breath, she mentally prepared herself for what she would need to do. She just needed to get through this night.

Shaking off the melancholy, Keelin hurried back to the

male who waited patiently where she'd left him, one hand resting on his tense thigh and the other still gripping the towel where it came together at his waist. She had a feeling he didn't take well to finding himself at such a disadvantage.

"I'm so sorry," she said, actually slapping her forehead this time. "I just realized I never even offered you something to drink or anything." Unfortunately, it was the hand that held the little plastic sewing kit. "Ow!"

Lucian chuckled as she rubbed the sore spot. "Let's just get this over with, an' then ye can fetch me a glass o' whiskey. If ye happen tae have some."

"I do. But are you sure you don't want that whiskey before I start? I have to admit I've never done this before."

"Nothin' tae it, lass. Just pretend yer mending a sock. Or a piece o' leather hide."

"A piece of leather hide," she mumbled. "Yeah. Okay. I can do that."

He glanced over his shoulder again, gray eyes shining with confidence in her. "Ye'll do fine, Keelin. I trust ye completely."

"Well, that makes one of us." She smiled at him with an air of calm she didn't feel as she sanitized the needle and thread with rubbing alcohol. The blood didn't bother her. It was the idea of purposely causing another creature pain she couldn't handle. Even if it was for their own good. "Well, at least it's an interesting way to meet someone new, isn't it?"

His shoulders shook as he let out a bark of laughter.

She took a deep breath. "Okay. Hold still." Her hand was surprisingly steady as she pushed the edges of the bite together and poked the needle through his skin. He was right. It *was* like sewing through leather. Warm, supple, smooth, leather.

Lucian didn't so much as twitch as she jabbed him with the needle. "So, how do ye ken?" he asked after a moment. "About what I am."

Keelin knew the question was coming, and yet, somehow, he still managed to take her by surprise. "Um. Well? Living up here in the mountains, you run into all kinds."

"Ye wouldn't have run in tae someone like me. Not without a verra good reason." He paused, and his shoulder muscles stiffened beneath her hands. "Have those things been here before?"

Things. Not Faeries. She shook her head, even though he couldn't see her. "No. Nope. That's the first time I've seen them here."

"Yet, ye dinna seem shocked tae see them. A little shook up, but no' shocked." He twisted his head around, eying her. "Ye dinna seem shocked now."

Keelin stared into those gray eyes, knowing where he was going with this, but unable to bring herself to lie. "I'm not shocked. Surprised, yes. *And* a little shaken. But not shocked." She paused, the needle hovering above his wound. "I'm very glad you showed up when you did."

He went back to staring at the wall, and Keelin breathed a soft sigh of relief. "So, ye ken what they are?"

Keelin resumed sewing his wound closed. "Yes. They were Faeries. Well, one of the tribes. Not all of them turn into those things."

He was silent for so long, she thought that would be

the end of it, but the twenty questions continued. "What were ye doin' in the woods, lass?"

She winced for him as she pushed the needle through a particularly tough spot. "I was taking a walk." That much was the truth. She often took to the woods to clear her head, no matter the time of day or night.

"At this time o' night?"

"Sure." She kept sewing, trying to think of something else to talk about that would distract him.

But she wasn't quick enough.

"Do ye always take walks in the woods at these ungodly hours? In the rain and the cold?"

Keelin was really beginning to wish she'd just let him run back up the mountain. "Uh, no. Not always. But sometimes. I had a hard day, and needed to clear my head. And it wasn't raining when I left."

He was quiet again. Long enough that she hoped he'd lost interest in this line of questioning for real this time. But he was persistent. "Ye never answered my first question, lass. How do ye ken about shifters? And the things ye found in the woods. How do ye ken about them?"

Keelin admitted to herself she'd made a mistake. She should've acted more shocked. But at the time, she hadn't even thought about it. She'd reacted honestly, like she always did. "My mom was a Wiccan. A witch. The good kind, ya know? She knew things other people didn't. She could see things." Well, that much was true at least. Although Keelin had no idea if Wiccans were Seers or not. But it sounded plausible.

"Human Wiccans dinna normally have tha' type o' sight."

Maybe not. "Well, my mom did." *Fake it till you make it, Keelin.* "Anyway, she knew about you guys. And she passed that knowledge down to me."

"Why?"

Keelin stopped what she was doing, thread pulled halfway through the loop that would form the end knot. "Why?" she repeated.

"Aye. Why would she share this knowledge with ye? A young girl."

"I'm not so young."

"Yer young enough. And were probably more so at the time she told ye. Most parents try tae protect their young from monsters, no' tell them they are real."

She finished tying the knot and snipped off the extra thread. Then she stood back, admiring her handiwork, trying her best to keep her breathing and heart rate calm. "Yeah, my mom was a bird of a different feather." The line of stitches looked good. And with his advanced healing powers, he'd be able to remove them later that day.

"A bird o' what?"

Keelin swabbed the wound with some alcohol and covered it with a bandage. Probably overkill. It's not like it would get infected. But she needed to keep her hands busy and her mind distracted. "It's just a saying," she told him. "Meaning she wasn't like other parents."

"Aye. I ken tha' much already." He tried to twist his head around to look at her handiwork. "All finished?"

"Aye," she teased. Then she pointed down the short hall toward her room. "The bathroom is down there, first door on your right, if you'd like to take a look and get dressed while I put this stuff away."

Lucian stood, gathering up the bundle of clothes with one hand and hanging onto his towel with the other. "I dinna suppose ye have any shoes tha' might fit me?"

Keelin raised one eyebrow. "Maybe some flip-flops? I'll look."

"Thank ye, lass. For the clothes, 'n' for stitching me up."

She smiled. "You don't have to thank me. You did save me, after all. It's the least I could do."

With a tight smile and a nod, Lucian wandered off to find her bathroom. Once he was gone, Keelin took a deep, steadying breath and began to gather up the odds and ends of her sewing kit and put it back together again. Back in her room, she shut the door and sat down on her bed with her head in her hands.

What the hell was she doing? What was she going to tell him? Because she knew for a fact that wolf was not going to go on his merry way before he got answers from her. And not just any answers. Answers he would be satisfied with. And she didn't have any of those kind of answers.

One thing was for sure. If she sat here wallowing in indecision, he'd come looking for her, and if he found her like this it would make him suspicious for sure. Standing up, she took another fortifying breath and went to the room next door to see if there was a pair of shoes that would fit him. She found a pair of slip-on Nike sandals and brought them out to the kitchen.

He was already dressed, standing in front of the sink, staring out the window. Keeping watch over her backyard? The clothes she'd loaned him didn't fit him well. They were, in fact, too small. The T-shirt stretched tight over the wide breadth of his shoulders and back, and the jeans were bulging at the seams and only made it down to the tops of his ankles.

They'd been a little too long on Brian.

Lucian turned from the window when she walked in. The light above his head caught the pale strands in his hair and the lines of stress around his mouth and eyes. "Ye did a fine job with the stitches, lass. Thank ye, again."

Keelin frowned. "You took off the bandage?"

"Aye. How else was I supposed tae see?"

He was so serious, she had to laugh. Then, to her surprise, he smiled too. The first true smile she'd seen from him. Some of the tension left the air.

"So," He leaned back against the sink and crossed his arms over his chest. Even in ill-fitting clothes, he was an imposing male. "Are ye gonna stop with the games 'n' fess up the answer tae my question? Or are ye gonna keep lying tae me?"

The air left Keelin's lungs and the smile slipped from her face. Thoughts bumped around in her head, one excuse after another. But in the end, she knew none of them would fool him. She raised her chin and opted for the only answer she could give him. "I'm going to have to choose the second option."

His eyes darkened.

"I'm sorry," she told him. And she was, truly. "But I can't say any more. For my own safety. And yours." Keelin suddenly realized she was freezing. She'd never bothered to change out of her wet clothes. Gooseflesh covered her skin and she started to tremble, small tremors that gradually escalated to a full-blown case of the shakes.

Lucian was beside her in a heartbeat, wrapping his big arms around her and holding her close to his heat. And wow, was he hot. Literally. This was something her mom had never bothered to mention. Or maybe she hadn't known this fact about shifters.

"It's okay, lass," he said. "Dinna fash yerself. It's all over now."

Keelin gripped the back of his shirt, unable to keep up the pretense while wrapped in the protective embrace of a stranger. "No, it's not," she whispered into his chest. "It hasn't even begun."

CHAPTER 3

Lucian tightened his arms around the lass as she shook violently in his hold, the feel of her soft curves chasing away the ugly thoughts he'd been having about exactly *whose* clothes he was wearing. Och. It shouldn't even matter to him. What did he care who she was shacking up with? But, it did. It bothered him a great deal. This wee human made him ache in ways he hadn't felt in a long, long time with one glance of her large, lonely eyes. Not since Sara. The she-wolf who'd ruined his life, and his relationship with his best friend.

However, wee or not, Keelin was hiding something. He'd felt it in his bones even before she'd admitted as much. But with a few whispered words into his borrowed shirt, she had him wondering who—or what—she really was.

She burrowed into his chest, and he relaxed on the next breath. This trembling female couldn't possibly be one of them. If she were, she would've used her Faerie magic to take out the things chasing her tonight. She wouldn't have needed him to intervene. She wouldn't be living here all on her own, among humans.

Still, a sour taste filled his mouth.

It hasn't even begun.

He kept his arms around her sweet curves, still wet, but warmer now from his body heat. "What do ye mean, lass? Those things are gone. Ye saw for yerself."

She stiffened in his arms and tried to pull away. Lucian released her, ignoring the way his body tried to follow her all on its own. Catching himself, he took a step back, frowning to hide his discomfort. It wasn't like him to be so soft when it came to females. He'd offered her comfort without thinking twice about it, and was loath to remove that comfort, even at her own insistence.

Keelin gave no indication that she thought his reaction odd. Her awkward laugh appeared to be aimed more at herself as she shook her head. "You're absolutely right." Then she scrubbed at her forehead with her fingers. "I'm sorry. I think the day is catching up to me is all."

Again, he got the feeling she was dancing quite a fancy jig around the real issue. The entire night just didn't add up to him. Not the part about the crazy Fae chasing her—although their drug of choice *was* humans, but what were they doing here?—or the part of how she'd taken it all in stride, more or less, and this being the first time this had happened. Supposedly. "Why do I get the feeling yer hiding more from me than yer tellin'?"

She shrugged, and looked him straight in the eye for the first time since she'd seen him. "Why do you care?"

The question was an honest one. She wasn't trying to

be crabbit about it. And Lucian realized she was right. Why *did* he care? "I dinna ken. But I do."

"Look," she continued, wrapping her arms around her waist. "I appreciate your help. More than you know. But there's nothing here you need to worry about. Truly. I'm fine now. Thanks to you." She smiled at him. A true smile that lit up her bonnie face. And later, lying in his own bed, Lucian would swear the heavens had opened up for a quick second before it was gone again. Keelin wasn't what one would consider a beauty, but her features were arresting in their purity, with a dash of sin that wouldn't let him take his eyes away. The curves of her body made perfectly for his hands.

She heaved a tired sigh. "Honestly, I just want to go to bed."

His cock jumped violently. Lucian snarled, more at himself than at her innocent words. Keelin expressing she was tired was *not* an invitation to join her, and he'd throat punch any eejit who took it as such. Including himself.

Shocked at his body's reaction, Lucian put a little more distance between them. He didn't know what the fuck was wrong with him tonight. Except that the thought of leaving this lass here alone, unprotected, filled him with foreboding. "I can stay, if ye'd like. No' in the house, o' course, but nearby, somewhere outside. I can keep watch for ye."

She immediately shook her head, her long hair brushing her shoulders and arms. He noticed it was lighter than he'd first thought, a tinge of red tinting the blonde strands as it dried. Her sweet scent wafted over to him, filling his lungs. It was tainted slightly. With fear?

"No. I couldn't ask you to do that. And it's really not necessary. I'll be fine." She paused, and mustered up another smile. "But thank you. Again."

That was his cue to leave. Yet, still, he hesitated. "I'm just no' comfortable leaving ye here alone. There might be more o' those bloody things out there."

"Well, if there are, I doubt they'll find me in my bed, right?"

How did she know that? "Aye, that's true. So long as they did no' ken where tae find ye in the first place." The infected ones, for whatever reasons, couldn't seem to sniff out their prey behind closed doors. Only if they ran into them out in the open. Unless, of course, they knew they were there. Then they would crash through brick and steel in their efforts to get their fix.

"Then, see? I'll be perfectly safe. Or as safe as any of the humans who live around here."

Try as he might, Lucian could think of nothing to say that would make her change her mind. For sure, he didn't even know why he was trying. This woman and her problems were not his concern. He needed to leave her be. "Aye. You're right. I dinna ken what I'm thinking." He took the shoes she was still holding. "Thank ye for the loan of clothes. I'll be sure tae get them back tae ye."

She unwrapped one arm and waved her hand in the air like she was trying to chase away bad memories. "That's not necessary. But if you could help me take care of the bodies out back, I'd be forever grateful."

"Och. O' course. I almost forgot. Dinna fash yerself, lass. I'll get rid o' them for ye afore the sun rises."

She was already walking toward the door. "I'll help you."

"Keelin."

She pulled up short at his tone.

Lucian joined her at the back door and made an effort to go easy on his tone of voice. "Go get some rest. I'll take care o' the bodies. Ye will no' even ken they were here. I promise ye."

He thought she was going to argue with him some more, but after an indecisive moment, she gave him a grateful smile. "Thank you, Lucian."

"Aye." He paused. "And dinna worry about any more unwanted visitors tonight. I plan tae stick around for a while an' keep an eye on things. Just in case. And dinna argue with me about it." Only to be assured there were no more soul suckers running amok on his mountains.

She looked up at him with eyes that raged with every shade of blue and green in the ocean. "You don't have to do that."

"I ken I dinna, but I will. I would no' feel right just leaving ye here without making sure ye were safe." To his utter amazement, he found those words to be true. With what he hoped was a reassuring smile, he slipped on the sandals and went out into the cold night, then stood on the small pack porch, waiting until she locked the door behind him.

After checking around carefully to make sure he wasn't being watched by anyone other than Keelin, Lucian gathered up the body parts. With a torso over each shoulder and a head in each hand, he jogged to the tree line and found a trail that would take him back up to the top. He hid the corpses in a clump of ferns, then found a sturdy branch to sit on. The tree was a good vantage point and afforded him some shelter if the rain came back—which it did, about two hours later. Despite the thick cover, he was quickly drenched. But a little rain never deterred him from his duty.

He kept watch until a few hours before dawn, and when he was assured there were no other soul suckers in the area, he gathered up the Fae corpses and hightailed it back through the mountains. He made it to the apartment building the pack shared just as the sun was peeking up over the horizon. The complex backed up to the protected lands of the mountain range, and provided plenty of cover for the werewolves to sneak in and out on occasions just such as this.

Questions tumbled over each other inside his head, mostly about Keelin, but he let them spin. He didn't want to think about why he'd felt the need to protect a female he'd just barely met. It would only lead to answers he was positive he didn't want to hear and wasn't ready to acknowledge.

Duncan met him on the elevator, dressed in sweats and running shoes. One eyebrow went up as Lucian stepped through the doors with the bodies. "Fun night ye had, eh?"

Och, he was not in the mood for Duncan this morning. Then again, he never really was. The wolf was a royal pain in the arse. Always nipping at his heals like an overgrown Chihuahua. Never leaving him alone. "Is Cedric awake?"

"I wouldn't ken. I slept in my own bed last night, as I do every night, and was just goin' out for a run."

Lucian rolled his eyes and continued down the hall-way. "I'll just go see for myself, then." He heard Duncan following him and spun in a circle as he walked to scowl at him. "Dinna ye say something about a run?" At Cedric's door, he tucked one of the heads beneath his arm and gave a right firm knock.

"Aye. And I will. But I dinna wanna miss *this* story."

Cedric opened the door right away, wearing nothing but black boxer briefs with a wadded up T-shirt in his hand, long hair yet to be pulled back into its customary ponytail. His icy blue eyes took in Lucian, the bodies, and Duncan in one fell swoop, before he stepped back and swung the door open wide. "Leave those things in the bath if ye dinna mind, Lucian. I dinna want Faerie guts all over my new floor. I'll make us all some coffee." Without a second glance, he shut the door behind them and made his way over to his recently updated kitchen, pulling the white T-shirt over his head as he went.

Lucian dumped the bodies in the guest bath, then washed his hands. His skin itched to be covered in his own clothes, and not because the ones he wore were too tight and too short, but because the thought of wearing another male's clothes—another male who meant some-thing to Keelin—made him want to rip them from his body. But Cedric would want to hear what happened first, so he settled with cleaning up as best he could and then followed the smell of strong, freshly-brewed coffee back out to the kitchen.

To his credit, Duncan said not a word about the ill-fitting clothing as he passed. "Are ye all right, lad?"

"O' course," Lucian sneered. He detested being called "lad". "There were only two o' them fer Christ's sake."

Cedric brought him and Duncan a steaming cup of coffee and then settled into his favorite oversized armchair with his own. He took a loud sip, closing his eyes and making an appreciative noise.

Lucian sat on the couch, Duncan beside him, as he waited.

Pushing his long, wavy hair out of his face, Cedric said, "All right, now that I can think straight, tell me what happened tae ye."

Lucian did, starting with the scene he'd come upon when he'd stopped at the top of the mountain cliff. He skipped over any details of what happened between him and Keelin he didn't need to know, only telling him her name and the main points of their conversation. He finished it up by saying she was a good, brave lass who'd fixed up his shoulder and loaned him some clothes.

"But she wasn't at all feart, ye say?" Cedric asked him when he was done.

"Not like ye would expect. She told me her mum was a Wiccan, 'n' a Seer, 'n' that she was the one who told her about the other creatures o' the world when she was a wee lassie."

"Creatures like us, ye mean?" Duncan said.

"Aye. 'n' the Faeries." He couldn't stop his upper lip from lifting in disgust.

Cedric set his coffee mug on the end table and sat forward in his chair. "So, let me get this straight. Ye saw a wee lass run out o' the woods when the moon was high, followed by a couple o' crazy ones, and ye did no' ask her what the bloody hell she was doing walking in the woods at night?"

"Och. O' course I did!" Lucian told him. "She claimed she likes tae go on late walks when it's quiet."

Cedric picked up his mug and stared down into his coffee. "What did ye say her name was?"

"Keelin Doran."

The pause was so brief Lucian almost didn't notice it. Almost. "That's a fine, Irish name."

"Aye," Lucian said. "That's what I told her." He glanced between Cedric and Duncan. "Why do I get the feeling there's more tae this lass than she's letting on? What are ye no' telling me?"

Duncan shook his head. "Yer imagining things."

"Are ye quite sure she said nothing else?" Cedric asked. "Ye dinna see anything unusual while in her home?"

"No, Cedric. Nothing. Though I do wonder why a sweet-smelling, bonnie lass like Keelin is living all alone in the middle o' fookin' nowhere."

"Sweet-smelling, ye say?" Duncan grinned at him.

But Lucian wasn't about to take the bait. "Aye. Like bog stars."

Cedric cleared his throat and nodded. "All right. Off with ye, then. Get a shower 'n' some sleep."

"What about the bodies in yer bath?"

"I'll have Prince Nada come 'n' fetch them. He'll want tae hear what happened." Cedric got up and took his empty mug over to the sink. "Come back down here after yer rested up, Lucian. 'n' I'll fill ye in on whatever I find out."

Duncan also took his cup to the sink. "I'm gonna go

ahead 'n' go on that run, then. Dinna kill anymore *an olc* without me, Lucian. 'n' aye, get that shower. Ye reek like a dead fish." With a wide grin, Duncan clapped him on the back and went out the door.

Lucian followed him out, taking the stairs up to his apartment rather than ride in the elevator with Duncan. He did reek. But not of fish. He smelled like those fucking Faeries. He would have to soak these clothes in bleach before he took them back to Keelin.

And take them back himself he would. Though it would be just as easy, and far safer, to find out her address and mail them to her, it didn't feel right to him. He wanted to check on her. Other than his obvious—and startling—attraction, something was nagging at him about that woman. And he was going to find out what it was.

Once he was clean and in his own jeans, hiker boots, and a green, button-down flannel shirt, he skipped the nap and headed straight back to Cedric's. Lucian didn't know exactly what it was that drove him, but there wasn't a thing he wanted discussed about Keelin without his ears being in on it.

At Cedric's, Lucian rapped twice on the door and waited for the alpha's command to enter. He hurried inside to find not only Prince Nada, but Princess Duana sitting on the couch across from Cedric. He had to bite back a growl at the sight of the Dark Fae princess before anyone noticed. Aye, she was bonnie enough, with her white skin and dark hair and curves, but it wasn't enough to make him trust her. She was *an olc*, a Dark Fae, an evil Fae. Not that the Good Fae were much better, as far as Lucian was concerned. Both tribes were devious, and they never fought fair, using their creepy Fae magic to get the advantage, even though they were nearly as strong as the wolves and could put up just as good of an honest fight.

Unless you got them close to iron. Aye. Iron took the piss right out of them.

At that very moment, Prince Nada stopped talking and looked right at him, a funny little smile slowly curving the corners of his mouth. With his long, white hair and fancy suit and cane, he reminded Lucian of a wizard in a movie he'd watched once. And just like in the movie theater, his hackles rose as he got the impression the prince knew exactly what he'd just been thinking.

Cedric spotted him hovering on the edge of the room and waved him inside. With a side-eyed look at the prince, Lucian made his way over to stand beside Cedric's chair. "What did I miss?"

"Ye did no' miss much," Cedric told him. "I just finished telling the prince 'n' princess what you found last night. They're in my bath, by the way," he said to Prince Nada. "I was thinking ye would want tae see them afore I got rid o' them."

"And you would be correct, sir," Prince Nada told him. The princess, on the other hand, did not seem so eager. He patted her shoulder. "You stay here, dear. I'll deal with this. We wouldn't want to upset your delicate sensibilities." He didn't see the amused look the princess gave him as he grabbed his cane and walked briskly toward the bathroom. "Didn't have much of a chance, did they?" he called.

"No' against my Lucian, no'," Cedric responded with a note of pride in his voice.

My Lucian. It was the first time Lucian had ever heard his alpha refer to him as such. And with such pride. His chest swelled at the compliment even as his face heated.

"Maybe Lucian can help me carry them out of here," Prince Nada said as he came back. "I'd prefer not to soil my suit."

Lucian gazed down at the clean clothes he'd just put on and ground his jaw.

The prince nodded at Duana when she looked up at him from her seat. "It's as we feared, dear."

Her expression didn't change, but her eyes were colored with betrayal when she turned back to Cedric.

"Dinna look at me like that, princess," he told her. "Lucian did right tae kill them. Ye ken tha' as well as I do."

"I don't 'ken' any such thing. As you well know," she spit.

"Put yer claws away, kitten. There no' much tae do about it now. The girl would've been killed before Lucian could've caught them alive, even if he'd tried tae. We cannae allow tha'."

"Because humans are so much more important?"

"Aye," he responded. "They are important. Just as important as any o' us."

His answer seemed to surprise her.

The prince pulled Lucian's attention away from their conversation. "Come help me, lad. Please."

But Lucian was already shaking his head. He already knew how the prince was planning to dispose of the bodies: by whisking them out of here through space and time to the gods only knew where. And he wanted to take Lucian with him. "No, I dinna think I will. I willnae be going with ye unless ye want me tae take them out the same way I brought them in."

"Lucian, go with the prince," Cedric ordered.

"I will no', Cedric," he ground out. There was no way in bloody hell he was letting that Faerie whoosh him from one place to another. "But I'd be more than happy tae take them out on my own two feet."

Cedric stood from his chair, and the timbre of the alpha weighed heavy on Lucian though his words were kind. "There's nothing tae be feart o', Lucian. I've done it myself many times now. Just go. I need ye back here."

His bravado was bullshit. Lucian knew Cedric hated it as much as he did. Though he had to clench his jaw to keep his mouth on lockdown before it got him into trouble—again—Lucian gave him a curt nod and brushed past the prince to go get the bodies.

He was going to have to bloody shower again.

CHAPTER 4

Once they were gone, Cedric sat back down and gave in to what he'd wanted to do since the moment she appeared at his door. He turned his full attention to Duana. She stared back at him with eyes dancing with color and an angry blush high in her cheeks. A sure sign of the state of her emotions even if the tension in the room hadn't gone up considerably. Though, at least on his own end of things, it wasn't their disagreement about her people causing it.

"You promised me you would give me the chance to help them," she said. Though her tone was even, and she spoke with that soft lilt he so loved, he could see it was an effort on her part not to scream at him, and not just by the rainbows swirling around in her eyes. Suddenly, she got up and began to pace back and forth behind the couch, further proving his point.

Today she wore black pants and a soft creamy sweater, both made of material that hugged her ample curves nearly as well as his hands would. Those boots all the girls wore the moment it got cold covered her feet. Mugs? Ugs? Och. He'd never be able to keep track of female fashion. Always changing. As for himself, he'd worn the same clothing for as long as he could remember—jeans, T-shirts or flannels, depending on the season, and low-cut black boots with thick soles. Today, it was flannel, as it was getting close to the winter solstice.

With some effort, he pulled his eyes away from her rounded arse and smoothed his hair back in its ponytail. There were more important matters to think about than the way her full breasts rose and fell with every angry breath. Cedric was near ashamed of himself, the way he ogled her every time she was near, like he was a flirt no better than Duncan. He needed to control himself. He was the alpha, and a male of honor.

But the female was more than a perfect collection of luscious curves. She was also willful, persuasive, and sharp as the words that came from her perfect lips. A challenge, to say the least.

His wolf practically purred like a feline in anticipation.

"Duana. Princess," he corrected. "I gave ye my word, 'n' I will keep it. This time just happened tae be a special situation. I was no' there, but from what he told me, Lucian did what he had tae do. I swear tae ye, the next time, we will no' kill them. At least no' until ye have a chance tae try tae…save them."

She stopped pacing and moved to stand before his chair. Cedric remained where he was, his eyes traveling slowly up her body. His cock swelled painfully, and not even the swift fluctuation of colors swirling in her eyes could change its mind. She inhaled deeply. But rather than calm her, the colors brightened. He liked to think it was because she was just as affected by him.

He was a fool.

"You don't think I can do it."

"I didnae say tha', lass."

"You didn't have to say it. Your expression and your tone say it all."

"Duana—" He reached a hand toward her.

But she'd already spun away, leaving him engulfed in her sweet scent. A groan caught in his throat.

She stopped near the couch again, her back to him. "No. It's all right if you don't believe in me. Honestly, I have to admit, I can't really blame you. If I were of a primitive species, I wouldn't be open to believing it, either."

Cedric rose from his chair. "Now, princess. There's no need tae be name-calling. Werewolves might be a wee bit passionate about things, 'n' sometimes we act more on instinct than our brains, but we are no' 'primitive'."

She turned, a smile playing around the edges of her mouth. One that didn't quite reach her eyes. "Forgive me. When I'm upset my mouth tends to say things before I think whether or not I should actually say it."

He noticed she didn't say she hadn't meant what she'd said. Only that she shouldn't have said it out loud. The urge to show her just how primitive he could be near overwhelmed him. So much so, he took a step toward her before he realized what he was doing and stopped himself. A low growl rumbled in his throat.

She raised one eyebrow, the smirk widening on her face.

"Dinna say a word," he grumbled. He scrubbed his face with his hands, wishing he had a bucket of ice water to stick his head in. To clear his thoughts. Actually, a full tub would be better. Stalking to the kitchen, he grabbed a Guinness out of the fridge. It was a wee bit early to be drinking, but at the moment, he didn't care. Cedric popped the cap off and dropped it in the trash, then took a long swallow. He decided to stay in the kitchen. Behind the counter. Where it was safe. "The human. The female Lucian saved. I'm concerned about her. Wha' she kens about us."

Duana narrowed her eyes as she crossed her arms over her chest. "Why?"

It was with the strength of the gods that he kept his eyes on hers, and not on the way her arms pushed her breasts toward the top of her sweater. Aye. She was watching him closely, searching for the slightest crack in his armor. Could it be she truly didn't know? "I just find it strange, tha' a human woman kens the things she does. About us. It worries me."

She dropped her arms, resting one hand on the back of the couch as she studied him. He must've passed her test, for a moment later she shrugged one shoulder. "I don't think she's anything to worry about. If what Lucian said is correct, she's known about us her entire life. And so what if she does?" she said after a pause. "There are a few humans who do."

Cedric took another swig of his beer, his mind spinning. She truly didn't know. But he did. And so did Duncan. Keelin Doran was no ordinary human woman.

As a matter of fact, she wasn't human at all.

Duana sighed, exasperation written all over her face. "If it makes you feel better, keep an eye on her. If you find any evidence that she's a threat, deal with her."

"Tha's pretty cold, princess."

She came toward him, stopping only when the counter between them would let her go no farther. "Yes. It is. Would you put your entire species at risk because of one human with a big mouth?"

"No," he told her without pause.

"Then you'll deal with her."

It wasn't a question, but he answered it all the same. "Aye, lass. I'll deal with her."

The smile that had been playing around her mouth earlier returned in full force. "Good. And if any more of my kind show up—"

"I'll take them alive," he finished. "For ye."

She stared at him as the colors dimmed in her eyes and they slowly returned to their normal shade. "Thank you, Cedric. It's our only chance, you know. We can't close the portal again even if we wanted to. The key is dead."

She was right. The one who had been able to close the portal to the world of the Dark Fae was gone. But if Lucian's story was true, and he had no doubt it was, all was not lost. Not yet.

Och. Why was she looking at him like that? "Dinna thank me yet, lass. I'm no' promising ye tha' I will nae kill them in the end."

"Just as long as you give me enough time to try to help them first." No longer roiling with the colors of her emotions, her rich brandy eyes were large in her wee face.

Too large. Mesmerizing. A trick of the Fae, he would swear to himself later.

Nevertheless, he was helpless captured in their depths. "Aye. I'll give ye a chance tae help them. But heed me when I say, I will no' risk the life o' any o' my pack. I will no' risk *yer* life, Duana." For her life was just as important to him, though at that moment, he truly could not say why.

"I would never ask you to," she told him.

Only it was more than mere words. It was a promise he felt in his gut. A promise that had nothing to do with his pack. A promise as strong as the connection he felt between them, pulling him closer to her across the width of granite, try as he might to fight it. His kitten had sheathed her claws. Not that it mattered. The fire in her blood aroused him like no other female before. "Duana…"

A loud noise came from the direction of the front door, and Cedric took a step back, breaking the spell as Lucian came crashing into his apartment.

He stomped into the kitchen, the blood of the dead spreading dark stains on his clothes, and glared at Cedric. "I will no' fucking do tha' again, Cedric! Do no' ask me tae!" Ripping open the door of the fridge so hard he nearly tore it from its hinges, he helped himself to a beer, popped the cap into the trash, and downed it all in four swallows. Chucking the bottle into the recycle, he grabbed another one and drank half of it before he wiped his mouth on his sleeve and parked it on a stool beside the princess.

Cedric knew he wasn't talking about disposing of the bodies. "'Tis a wee bit disconcerting," he agreed.

In response, Lucian glared at him and chugged his beer.

Prince Nada appeared out of thin air on Duana's other side as Cedric got two more beers and set one in front of Lucian. The prince grinned. "Yes, I would like a drink. A nice Irish whiskey, if you please."

"We have beer," Cedric told him. "But it *is* Irish." He grabbed another Guinness and popped the cap for the prince, setting it in front of him.

"Ah, that'll do just fine." The prince took a dainty sip, pulling a square of linen from an inside breast pocket and dabbing the corners of his mouth.

Cedric leaned over the counter, glancing surreptitiously over at Duana, who was engaged in a game of "tease the big, bad, wolf" with Lucian for being afraid of something as minor as Faerie travel. He kept his voice low, barely above a whisper. "She does no' ken about the girl Lucian found." He didn't need to specify what "she" he was talking about.

"No," the prince said just as quietly, and took another sip of his beer.

"Did *ye* ken about her?"

The prince frowned. "I may have heard something…"

"We need tae protect her. If she is discovered—"

Prince Nada gave him a strange smile. "She can protect herself."

"Aye," Cedric agreed. "But I would feel better if we made sure o' that."

The prince wandered over to the large window on the other side of the sitting area and Cedric followed him. "I was thinking, as he is already taken with her, tha' Lucian could keep an eye on her for a time."

"And how will you explain the need to Lucian?"

"I'll tell him it's tae make sure no more o' the soul eaters come sniffing around the woman, or anyone else in the area." Cedric took a long pull from his bottle as he stared out at the trees. "We need tae protect her. Without her, we cannae contain what is coming."

"If it will make you feel better to have one of your dogs keeping watch, by all means, go ahead. It certainly wouldn't hurt."

"Then we are agreed?"

"Yes, wolf. We are agreed."

They exchanged a weighted look, and for once, the prince actually appeared to share his concern, despite his flippant way. Cedric finished his beer and strode across the apartment to throw it away and save Lucian from Duana's sharp tongue.

CHAPTER 5

Keelin stepped from the shower, wrapping a thick towel around her long hair. After the excitement of the night before, she'd had a hard time getting to sleep. And as a result, she'd overslept that morning and was late for work. So, she'd twisted her hair up into a bun, threw on some clothes, and ran out the door without even taking the time to tie her boots. She'd even forgotten her coffee, which hadn't made for a productive morning. Or afternoon, for that matter.

The only saving grace to her day was how much Keelin loved her job. The local Sauk-Suiattle tribe had been a bit reluctant at first to hire her as assistant to Eddie Morris, their Silviculturist. But, somehow, she'd managed to convince them to give her the job. Not only did it help Keelin pay the bills, but it allowed her to do what she loved most: take care of the forests in the area. Although mostly she worked in the nursery and conducted research on tree growth rate, duration of seed viability, and the effects of fire and animal grazing, among other problems of forest propagation, she got to have her hands in the earth and her heart in tune with nature. She didn't think she would've gotten through Brian's death if she'd had to work as a waitress or retail clerk or some other mundane job. She didn't have the patience for people'ing on a good day. But working in the forest, Keelin felt right at home in her new life in Darrington, WA. The Native American culture was very similar to her own when it came to their feelings about mother earth.

At least, she *had* enjoyed living there, until Lucian Kincaid had shown up in her backyard.

An image of him standing in her kitchen, naked as the day he was born, flashed through her head. All thick muscle and righteous anger, even when he appeared calm. Not everyone would notice, but Keelin could feel it, like a volcano simmering just beneath the surface. Ready to explode any moment.

She wondered briefly what it would be like to have all that rage channeled into something else. Something like lust. What would it be like to have that fire ignite? Would it keep her warm?

Or burn her to ashes?

Keelin shook her head hard. Those were dangerous thoughts to have about that particular male. And she would be an idiot to forget that. Though she'd heard many tales from her mom before she'd died, last night had been the first time she'd actually witnessed the brute strength of a werewolf.

It was awesome.

And terrifying.

Remembering the ease with which he'd torn apart the two Fae, it suddenly hit her how easily he could do the same to her. The realization hit her hard, and it took her three tries to tie her blue bathrobe closed because her hands were shaking so. Bracing them on either side of the sink, she stared down the drain, imagining the pieces of her life—pieces she'd meticulously connected into something brand new and simple—slipping down the slimy pipes, only to come crashing out the other end, broken and scattered and drowning in sewage.

Of all the wolves who could've come to her "rescue", why the hell did it have to be *Lucian Kincaid*? She would've preferred anyone else. Even the alpha, Cedric. He had a fierce reputation, but was also known to be tolerant of others and a fair judge of character. Surely, he hadn't gained that reputation for no reason. The one called Duncan, from what she'd heard, could've been won over with a smile and a wink and a little cleavage. Marc and Brock were rumored to be wrapped around the fingers of their own Fae females, and, she would like to think, have become more sympathetic to others of their kind.

But Lucian? Lucian was known for his quick mind, his explosive temper, and his hatred of the Fae. Not a promising combination where Keelin was concerned. If he discovered what she was, it would all be over.

Someone knocked on her back door as she was pulling the towel off her head. Keelin froze and stared at her reflection in the mirror in disbelief. She didn't have to look outside to see who it was. She knew who was standing on her porch.

Lucian.

For one, anyone else would be at her front door, as was custom. For two, she felt his nearness like a physical thing, even though she had yet to lay eyes on him. Her heart began to pound so hard in her chest her head swam, and she had to hold onto the wall so she wouldn't end up on the floor. What was he doing here? What did he want? She thought back to the night before, frantically searching for clues as to why he would come back. Maybe he was just returning the clothes she'd loaned him as he'd said he was going to. Surely, there was no need to panic. If he'd come to hurt her, or worse, he wouldn't be knocking on the door.

Quickly, she ran her fingers through her long, damp hair and hurried down the hall and through the kitchen. A peek out the window confirmed it was the wolf she'd met last night, looking good enough to eat in a blue flannel shirt and jeans that were *just* tight enough. A wavy lock of his dark red hair fell over his forehead, and he pushed it back with an impatient gesture. Keelin noticed he did, indeed, have a paper bag in one hand. Most likely with Brian's clothes.

She glanced down to make sure her robe was still closed, then unlocked the door and opened it just enough to stick her face out. The temperature had dropped rapidly with the setting sun, and she smelled snow on the air. Keelin schooled her expression into a polite smile. "Hello again."

Lucian shifted his weight back and forth, his tongue wetting his lower lip as he took in her short bathrobe. He appeared nervous, though she didn't know what the hell he had to feel nervous about. But she reconsidered that assumption as his eyes traveled down the length of her wet hair to the "V" of her robe, where the curves of her breasts were clearly visible. They rested there a moment too long, and Keelin had to force herself not to pull her robe closed like a nun.

When they returned to hers, she almost stepped back from the hunger darkening them. "Do ye mind if I come in, lass? It's right freezing out here and I dinna want ye tae catch a chill."

Shivers chased each other along the surface of her skin at the sound of his deep voice. She shouldn't be noticing his voice—deep and rusty—or anything else for that matter. But he was a hard male not to notice. And not only because he could snuff her from existence at any moment. Keelin paused, her mind screaming at her to slam the door and run. Instead, she stepped back and opened it wider, the smile frozen on her face. "Of course, come on in."

He stepped inside, eyes narrowing on her as he passed. As she closed the door, he lifted his nose to sniff the air before he turned and handed her the bag. "Here are the clothes ye let me borrow. I washed the Fae stink out o' them for ye."

She took the bag and set it on the kitchen table, taking the opportunity to relax her features before she turned back to him. "Thank you, but that wasn't necessary. And it was the least I could do." When he didn't leave, but stood there awkwardly, looking anywhere but at her, she asked, "Is there something else you needed?"

His eyes snapped to hers, stormy and intense, and Keelin felt the breath whoosh out of her lungs. The urge to pull her robe tighter around her body was strong, but she fisted her hands in her pockets and resisted the impulse. She did, however, take a step back, putting some much-needed distance between them so she could breathe again. Closing her eyes, she sucked in air, silently scolding herself to get a grip.

When she opened them again, he was still staring at her.

He cleared his throat. "There is something else," he said. "I told Cedric, my pack leader, what happened here last night. He's concerned, as am I, and—if it's all right with ye—he would like me tae hang around a while tae protect ye. In case the fookers come back."

By an act of the gods, Keelin managed to keep the panic off her face. "I don't need a bodyguard, but thanks for the offer."

He studied her. "Ye dinna have tae be feart o' me, lass. I would never hurt ye."

"I'm not afraid of you," she lied. Keelin's mind spun as she tried to figure out what his game was. It wasn't like the wolves to care this much about one human. Something else was going on here. "That's not the only reason, is it?"

The corners of his mouth turned up just a bit. "No. It's no' the only reason. He also wants tae keep tabs on ye, being that ye ken so much about us."

Dammit. Keelin's heart fluttered in her chest, and she knew he heard it by the way he tilted his head and refocused his attention on her. She unclenched her fists within the pockets of her robe, willing her body into a state of calm, lest he hear the pounding of her pulse.

"That's really not necessary. I've known about your kind since I was a kid. If I was going to use that knowledge to put your pack in any kind of danger, I would have done something to that effect that by now, don't ya think?"

He took a step toward her. A hunter feeling out his prey. "Maybe ye just haven't found the right opportunity tae do it."

She laughed, the sound too loud even in her ears, giving away her nervousness. "That's absurd. Why would I tell anyone about you? Especially knowing what would happen to me if I did. I'm not stupid."

"Why does anyone do anything?"

He was close now. Too close. One of the kitchen chairs pressed against her ass and thighs. She didn't even realize she'd retreated as he'd advanced until she felt the press of wood. But she refused to run, no matter how nervous he made her. She was trapped. Besides, she had the distinct feeling that running would be a very bad idea, unless she wanted to be chased. And caught. "I swear I wouldn't do that. I'm not stupid. It would be a death sentence."

He smiled then, and the sight of it chilled her through to her bones. "Maybe no' a death sentence, but we would have tae be sure ye couldn't tell anyone else, ye ken?"

"Yeah. I 'ken'." Sliding out from between him and the table, she walked over to the stove and put the teakettle on. Her hands shook, and water sloshed out onto the stove. She kept talking to try to distract herself. "So, what? I have a wolf watching my every move for the rest of my life? That would be a little inconvenient for everyone involved." More than that, it would mean she wouldn't be able to run. Find a new place. A new life. Leave this one behind, along with all of its bittersweet memories. She should've left today. She should've pretended to go to work and ran. She could've been in a new place by now, with a new identity.

"I dinna ken. I only ken what Cedric told me tae do for now."

Keelin busied herself getting her teacup ready and forced herself to think about this logically. She wasn't in any immediate danger. At least not yet. And having the wolves hanging around maybe wouldn't be so bad. She didn't want to leave this life, yet. She liked it here. She liked her house. She liked her job. She liked being where she could still feel Brian with her. She wasn't ready to leave him behind. Not yet.

As if he knew where her thoughts had taken her, Lucian pointed with his chin to the bag on the table. "Who do I have tae thank for the loan?"

Keelin opened her mouth to answer him, but the words she had planned to say wouldn't come. She wrapped her arms around her waist to hold in the pain. "They belonged to…someone who used to live here with me." She didn't know why she was so reluctant to tell him whose clothes he'd borrowed. It was painful to talk about, yes. But she'd always managed to get the words out before. She cleared her throat and forced her voice to work. "They belonged to my boyfriend, Brian. But…he's gone now."

She prepared herself for more questions. Everyone always asked more questions. But Lucian must have read something in her expression that others couldn't see or didn't bother to notice. His mouth pressed into a hard line and he dropped his chin to his chest. In sympathy? Sorry he asked? It was hard to tell.

Surprisingly, the fact that he hadn't asked made it easier for her answer. "He killed himself." The words came out as barely more than a whisper. "I came home from work and found him in bed, two empty pill bottles and a note on the table beside him." Now that she was talking she found she couldn't stop. "He said he was sorry, and that I shouldn't blame myself." Keelin almost laughed. The night before his death, she had confessed to him who she was. *What* she was. She'd thought he'd be able to handle it. But Brian had had issues before she came along, and though he'd appeared to be in a good place since they'd met, she'd apparently underestimated the depth of his illness.

Or maybe she'd underestimated his ability to handle finding out what exactly he'd been sleeping with for the past seventeen months.

"He was seeing a doctor." She gave him a weak smile. "I don't think it was helping." She took a deep breath. "He was a wonderful man, and though I only knew him for about a year, I loved him very much." This was the most Keelin had talked about Brian's suicide since the day she'd found him lying in their bed. She'd switched bedrooms, gotten rid of their bed and bought a new one, but couldn't bring herself to move back into that room or get rid of any of his things.

Lucian didn't say any of the stupid things people usually said when they first found out. He didn't offer her any fake sympathy, didn't tell her it wasn't her fault. He just stood there, offering her comfort by his presence alone, sharing his strength with her.

Keelin felt it like a physical thing, seeping through her pores and steeling her up. She took another deep breath. "Anyway, it's a good thing I still had his clothes lying around."

"Aye, it was. If ye didn't, my bare arse running off tae the woods would've given the neighbors enough gossip tae blather about for a year, at least."

It took her a few seconds for the humor to hit her. Keelin laughed. It felt good to laugh. "Well, they probably need a little excitement in their lives."

He smiled again, and this time it actually reached his eyes.

Keelin sobered as she stared at him.

The male was savagely beautiful.

But before she could get her fill of that smile, it gradually fell away. "Ye still miss him."

The answer came without thought or hesitation. "All the time."

He gave a nod, breaking eye contact, and somehow she had the feeling her words affected him more than he was letting on.

It was time for a change in subject. "So, do I have a choice in any of this?"

He gave her a puzzled look.

"About the bodyguard situation."

"Och, no, Keelin. I'm afraid ye dinna. I have my orders, 'n' I have tae obey them."

She took a deep breath and looked around her kitchen.

"Well, then it looks like I have a dinner guest. I'll just go get dressed and find us something to eat."

He put a hand on her waist as she went to pass, stopping her. "Ye dinna have tae do all that. I just wanted tae alert ye tha' I'll be lurking around."

The heat of his palm burned straight through her fluffy robe to the bare skin beneath. Keelin's pulse began to pound, and a pool of warmth spread from where he touched her, stealing along her skin until her entire body felt feverish. A deep ache began to pulse in her lower belly. One she hadn't felt in a long time. All from a simple touch.

Lucian's burning eyes latched on to hers and a muscle jumped in his jaw, he was clenching his teeth so hard. But he didn't pull his hand away. Instead, his fingers curled, bunching the soft material of her robe into his fist.

They stood like that for what seemed an eternity, caught in the spell of each other, until, with a low growl, Lucian finally unclenched his hand and released her robe. He took a step back, and his voice, when he spoke, was rough. "I'll be just outside if ye need me." Then he turned on his heel and marched out the back door.

Keelin stood where she was, willing her breathing to return to normal. She looked around her kitchen, staring at the white counters and cabinets like she'd never seen them before.

What the hell had just happened?

She glanced at the door where Lucian had just disappeared, her hand to her throat. Blinked a few times. Then she gave herself an internal shake and hurried to her room to get dressed before she gave in to the urge to follow him.

CHAPTER 6

Snow was beginning to fall when Lucian left the warmth of Keelin's home, but it did nothing to cool his heated blood. Gripping the railing, he barely felt the crumbling shards of ice biting into his fingers as he stared off at the trees in the distance. Emotions coursed through him and things filled his head. Things he wanted to do to a woman he barely knew. Erotic things he hadn't thought about in a very long time.

Erotic and disturbing, because they involved being close to her. And if he got close, he would start to care. Lucian had no desire to care that much about anyone ever again. Bad things happened to people he cared about.

Memories flashed through his head. Pictures of his parent's bodies in grotesque positions, partway shifted until they were half human and half wolf, eyes wide and unseeing in death. He and Brock had been playing down by the loch when it happened. Fucking playing. Without a care in the bloody world. The entire pack gone when they returned to their village. The *entire pack*. Slaughtered by dark magic.

He closed his eyes as the memory came rushing back, clear as if it had happened yesterday, making his chest ache.

"Ye fookin' cheated!"

"I did no'!"

"Aye, ye did! Ye bastard." Lucian braced his hands on his knees near the entrance to the fort he and his best friend, Brock, had spent the entire summer clearing. It was their favorite place. They came here everyday to get away from the endless drama of a pack full of hot-blooded werewolves.

Lungs heaving with much needed air, he looked out over the blue water of the loch to the green hills in the distance. Their newest project—a raft made of fallen logs they'd hauled in from miles away and tied with rope they'd nicked from the merchant —sat at the edge of the water. As soon as they felt brave enough, they planned to test it out on the water, and search for the ancient sea creature his father insisted lived there.

"It's no' my fault yer slower than the sap tha' runs from the trees," Brock teased him, his voice already deeper than Lucian's own. "I beat ye every time, Lucian. Ye might as well give it up."

Lucian punched him in the shoulder. "Aye. Because ye fookin' cheat!"

With a whoop, Brock tackled him, and Lucian laughed as they tumbled head over arse down the embankment. They landed in a pile of dirty breeches and sweaty arms and legs, both of them laughing too hard to take it any further.

Brock rolled off to the side and pushed himself up on his

elbows. A long hank of brown hair fell over his eye. "We need tae get back. Yer maw will have us by the ears if yer late for dinner again."

He was right. The sun was already behind the green and purple hills. "And yer maw will paddle yer arse!" Lucian grinned.

"Aye, that she will," Brock agreed with a grin as he sat up and shoved his hair out of his face.

Lucian pushed himself off the ground and dusted off his pants, then helped Brock cover the secret entrance to their fort. They'd discovered the nature-made shelter at the beginning of the summer—a cave created when a fallen tree had fallen into a group of other trees. They'd cleared the ground beneath, and added more logs and brush until it was thick enough to keep out the frequent mist and rain. The door they'd made from weaving sticks and leaves kept animals from taking it over when they weren't there. Deep as it was in the shadows of the trees, it wasn't obvious to anyone who might pass by. All of which made it the perfect hiding spot.

They started walking back toward their village, talking with their heads together and making plans for launching the raft the next day. The wind picked up and the temperature dropped as nightfall encroached. It was going to be a full moon that night, and before long, the hills would be crawling with the wolves of their pack. Howls would lull Lucian to sleep that night, as he dreamed of the day he, himself, would be big and brave enough to run wild across the hills, hunting creatures weaker than he and protecting the pack from its enemies.

Screams pierced the night, the terrifying sounds filtered through the trees as a bright light lit up the sky ahead, jarring Lucian from his daydreams.

"What the fook was tha'?" Lucian looked at Brock, but his best friend was staring toward their village, eyes wide and mouth slack with shock.

"Brock! What was tha'?"

Snapping out of it, Brock grabbed Lucian by the hand. "We need tae hide, Lucian. Come on. Run!"

But he shook off Brock's hand. "No! We cannae run. We need tae go help our families!"

"Dinna be daft, Luc! We're fookin' pups. We have no' even started shifting, yet. Hell, I should no' even be saying 'fook', yet. I dinna think there's anything we can do! The elders will handle whatever tha' was. We need tae hide!"

Lucian broke out into a run, shouting over his shoulder, "I'm no' abandoning my family!"

"Lucian!"

Soon, Brock's footsteps sounded close behind him. Lucian knew he would catch up. Brock had longer legs. It was why he always won their races. As they approached the edge of their village, Brock caught him by the shoulder and yanked him back behind one of the elder's small houses. They pressed their backs against the wood, breathing quietly through their mouths as they'd been taught. An acrid smell burned the back of Lucian's throat and brought water to his eyes. Heart racing with fear, he stepped around Brock.

He needed to find his family.

"Wait. Wait!" Brock whispered, grabbing him by the wrist. "We cannae just run in there. We dinna ken what's happened or who's here. Or if anyone is still..." He didn't finish what he'd been about to say. But he didn't have to.

Lucian shook off his hand, but remained where he was, listening for sounds of intruders. All he heard was the wind swaying in the trees and the nightingales calling their mates home for the night. "I can no' just stand here. I have tae ken where my maw and da are. And my sister. What if something terrible is happening tae my sister?" He'd heard the males in the pack and how they talked about the things that happened to she-wolves who lost the fight. His sister was older and had already gone through the change. She would've fought alongside his parents.

The thought pushed him forward. "I'm going. Come with me or stay here. I dinna care." Ducking low, he kept to the sides of the buildings as he made his way through the village. Brock stayed close on his heals, just like Lucian knew he would do. They saw nothing and no one in the encroaching twilight. Their home was like a ghost town.

Near the center of the village, they stopped. The door to the council lodge had swung open in the wind. As the boys watched, it tried to shut again, but something was blocking the doorway.

Lucian crept closer, Brock one step behind him with a hand on his shoulder. A large wolf lay in the doorway, half in and half out of the building, partially covered in dark red fur.

The color exactly like Lucian's own.

The scream ripped from his throat without thought or warning as Lucian ran toward his father's half-shifted body, not caring who would see him or what might befall him. He dropped to his knees beside the body of the wolf, pounding his fists on his da's chest. "No...no. Wake up. Da! Please, wake up!"

Brock's shoulder bumped his as he landed beside him. "Lucian. Why is he like this? He's only half shifted!"

Lucian couldn't answer him. He didn't know why his da hadn't changed back when he'd died, and he didn't fookin' care. Gripping the thick fur around his father's neck, Lucian buried *his face in the half-wolf's chest, tears falling freely as sobs wracked his narrow chest. Vaguely, he heard Brock inhale sharply and felt him brush his arm as he rose to his feet. But Lucian couldn't tear himself away from his father's body.*

A horrified wail soon filled the increasing darkness. Brock. Lucian sucked in a staggering breath, and with one last look at his father, he went to find his friend. Following the sounds of grief through the village, he found more wolves scattered around the village in various stages of shifting. The entire pack was gone. Dead. His mind felt foggy, like he was caught in some type of nightmare he couldn't wake from, and he nearly stumbled over his maw's body. His sister lay near her. Both nude. His sister's hands were paws, her legs twisted perversely beneath her, her developing breasts partially hidden with fur. His maw was still mostly in human form. The hackles rose on the back of his neck. There was no blood. No signs of a fight. Only dead wolves.

A lingering current of dark magic tickled the hair on his arms and made his head tingle. Only one creature he knew of could cause something like this to happen.

Throwing back his head, he screamed his rage and grief at the moon.

YEARS LATER, adopted into a new pack, his best friend was beaten to within an inch of his life and banished. He'd taken the blame for something Lucian had done, and coward that he was, Lucian could not bring himself to confess the truth. That it was he, Lucian, who had lured the she-wolf Sara from her mate—an unforgivable offense. Not Brock. Instead, he'd just let it happen. He'd destroyed a lifelong bond for a female. Shortly after, Sara had gone back to another male. He'd waited, thinking she was just frightened, upset over the consequences of what they'd done. But then Sara and her mate had had a child together.

Their bond was sealed.

After that, every day became more miserable than the last. Lucian stayed as long as he could, but after a time, he couldn't bear it anymore. Watching them together, day in and day out. The happy, fucking family. The family that was supposed to be his. And so, he'd left.

He'd survived on his own for a while, mostly out of sheer stubbornness and anger. And then he hadn't. Lost and alone and angry at the world, he'd given up. That was when Cedric had found him. Confronting Lucian's violent thrashing about with naught but a raised eyebrow, the pack master brought him into his home and into his pack, and though Lucian knew a wolf on his own was as good as a death sentence, he hadn't been exactly grateful. Even now, at times, he couldn't stop himself from challenging the alpha. Cedric didn't deserve the attitude Lucian gave him, he knew that. Yet, he couldn't seem to stop himself. All of the anger and frustration he'd lived with for so long was always right there, just below the surface, and more often than not, it would shoot out of his mouth without warning.

Thing was, Lucian didn't even know why he was so angry. Not anymore. Yeah, he'd been handed some shite deals in his life. But others have gotten a lot more and still managed to walk through life with a smile.

Look at Brock. If anyone had a reason to be bitter, it was Brock. They'd grown up together, best friends all of their lives, and Lucian had thrown him to the wolves. Quite literally. After Brock was banished, Lucian had lain awake nights wondering where he was, how he was doing, if he'd found others of their kind, if he were alive...or dead. He'd even thought about going after him once or twice. But could never get his limbs to follow through with his brain's orders. Over time, the urge had faded, but he never stopped thinking about him. Wondering.

When he'd found out Brock was not only alive, but in Seattle, Lucian had felt such a sense of relief he'd nearly passed out. But that feeling was followed by a surge of guilt that weighed on him so heavily he couldn't breathe. But the bitter anger buried beneath it pushed its way back to the surface, saving him.

Imagine his surprise when, after a heart to heart in Cedric's apartment, Brock forgave him for everything.

His brother had a big heart. Accepted everyone. Lucian, however, still had one major issue with his friend —his Faerie mate.

How Brock could fall for one of them, Lucian would never know. They weren't to be trusted. She might seem fine now, but just look at their prince! Prince Nada was bloody mad. You never knew what he was thinking, and even when he told you, he made no fucking sense. Lucian didn't know if he'd always been like that, or if all the Fae magic flowing through him had fried his brain.

It wouldn't surprise him if it was Heather's Faerie magic that had Brock under her spell.

Lucian's mouth twisted into a scowl. It wouldn't surprise him if they were all under some kind of spell— Brock, Marc, and even Keegan, the Texas pack leader. If that male could fall for a Fae lass after using her for livestock in his Rodeo, what other explanation could there be?

The door opened behind him, and he tensed. Not from fear. But from something far more terrifying to him.

"Please come in and eat with me," Keelin said. "And I made up the bed in the spare room for you. If you're going to insist on staying here, I'll never get any sleep thinking about you out here freezing in the snow."

He turned and opened his mouth to refuse. But one look at her in her flannel pants and thick socks, with a black sweater pulled tight against the cold, her face pinched with worry as she glanced around at the falling snow, and he shut it again. With a nod, he joined her inside again. "Thank ye, verra much. I would appreciate a meal." Lucian didn't mention the bed. Just the thought brought visions of her on it, honey hair spread across his pillow, curvy legs wrapped around his waist.

His cock swelled until he felt he was about to burst from his jeans, and he discreetly adjusted himself while she went over to the stove. He must've been out there longer than he thought, for there was something boiling on one of the burners, and a wonderful smell came from the oven. A loaf of fresh bread sat on a cutting board on the counter, knife beside it. Lucian picked it up and began to slice the bread in a desperate attempt to keep his eyes and hands off of the woman.

Keelin spoke, slightly behind him and to his left. "I'm just heating up some leftover roast and gravy, and I've got some potatoes boiling. I hope that's okay."

"'O' course. It smells verra good. I'm grateful for whatever ye have."

She set the table while he finished slicing the bread, adding a bottle of red wine and two glasses. Soon after the roast and potatoes were ready. Lucian was careful not to accidentally touch her as he helped her put the food on the table, afraid if he did so he wouldn't be able to stop himself a second time from kissing her.

Scents filled his nose and his mouth began to water. Whether from the smell of the meal or the thought of kissing her sweet mouth, he couldn't say. Out of habit, Lucian went for the chair on the far side of the table, where his back would be against the wall. Keelin came at it from the other side. She stopped when she noticed him there, a small smile of apology turning up the corners of her mouth.

"I apologize," Lucian told her. "Ye take it, lass." As she sat down, he took the next best seat, facing the door. He found it interesting that she, a human, felt the need to sit where nothing could sneak up on her.

Or, perhaps he was overthinking it. Maybe she just liked that chair.

He offered her some potatoes before piling them up on his own plate. Though they both put on appearances, as though this were nothing but a casual dinner, the tension in the air was so thick it made his hackles stand on end.

Lucian wasn't good at casual conversation, but he made an effort to put her more at ease. "So, tell me more about yerself, Keelin."

She handed him the fork for the roast. "I think you already know plenty about me."

It was a habit of hers, he'd noticed, shutting down questions without a proper answer. But Lucian was not to be deterred. "Do ye work? Or did some distant relative leave ye all o' this?" He indicated the house they were in.

"I work," she said around a mouthful of bread. "I bought this house a few years ago when I moved to the area."

Lucian waited, and when nothing else was forthcoming, he asked, "What is it that ye do?"

She glanced over at him, taking his measure. He tried to look only mildly curious, so as not to give her a reason to shut him out. But he could see the wheels spinning in her head, wondering if giving up this information would tell him more than what he absolutely needed to know about her.

She was a mystery, this one. One he felt the need to solve even if Cedric hadn't insisted.

"I'm an assistant to the local Silviculturist."

Somehow this didn't surprise him. "You preserve the forests." He shoved a mouthful of roast dripping with gravy into his mouth.

She looked surprised that he knew. "Yes. Exactly."

"Aye. We need more people like you, lass. Most humans could give a shite about our planet. I dinna ken why we bother keeping them around."

She stared at him for a few seconds, fork lifted halfway to her mouth. "Um...Because then we wouldn't have Netflix?"

His face heated. He'd forgotten who he was having dinner with. "Och. I apologize. I should no' have said that."

"It's okay," she told him with a shrug. "Most of the time I agree with you."

They finished their meal in relative silence. Every once in a while he would glance over at her to find her watching him with a funny expression on her wee face. But she would drop her eyes and say something unimportant before he could think much of it.

When Lucian couldn't eat another bite, he sat back with a sigh. "Thank ye, lass. I haven't eaten tha' well in a long time."

"You don't know how to cook?"

"Aye. I do. Just no' tha' good."

She stood and started collecting the dishes and Lucian got up to help her, taking them over to the sink as she started washing. Reaching around her, his chest brushed her shoulder as he placed the empty plates in the water. Heat raced over his skin, though it was only their clothes that had brushed. He stayed, one hand still on the dish in the sink, unwilling to move away.

Keelin froze, both hands submersed in the soapy water. Her chest rose and fell rapidly, and he could hear her heart racing fast as a bird. She turned her head, her eyes at a level with his chest, before she slowly raised them to his.

Lucian searched the blue-green depths, looking for a sign that he should move away. He saw none. Without thinking much about what he was doing, he reached up and shut off the water.

Keelin swallowed visibly, her eyes never leaving his face.

He dipped his head, hesitating, waiting for her to pull

away. When she didn't, he did what he'd been thinking about since he'd first seen her standing in the rain.

At first, it was just the lightest sweep of his lips on hers. Barely a taste. Her mouth was soft and pliant, her breath sweet from the wine, and with the tip of his tongue, he tasted a little bit more, running it along her full lower lip.

Keelin moaned low in her throat, the sound primitive and filled with need.

It was his undoing.

Trembling with the effort it took to contain the beast howling in his blood, Lucian turned her to him as he nipped at her lower lip. Her wet hands came up to press flat against his chest, soaking his shirt. Taking her face between his palms, he deepened the kiss as her hands fisted, trying to pull him closer, but Lucian resisted her. He was afraid if allowed her closer, he would have her on her back on the dirty kitchen floor, such was his sudden and urgent need for this woman. And she deserved better than to be rutted upon like a dog.

Her tongue touched his, tentative at first, dragging him from his thoughts. Lucian stilled, so as not to frighten her, but couldn't stop his hands from sliding from her face to the warmth beneath her sweater. As she grew bolder, he gripped the sides of her shirt, the back of his knuckles pressing into the soft flesh of her sides, fighting the need to pull her soft curves into his body.

Lucian growled deep in his throat as the kiss grew beyond his control. His muscles, taut and shaking, burned with the need to sink into her. His cock felt like it was going to explode in his pants. But all he could do was kiss her. He couldn't get enough of the taste of her.

Blood roared in his ears as she rose on her toes and pulled against his hold, leaning into him. Her hardened nipples brushed his chest. Lucian growled deep, his skin too tight for his frame.

Bones shifted beneath the taut muscle. Just slightly. But it was enough to jar him from the haze of lust. With an act of will he didn't know he possessed, he tore himself away. Taking three steps back, he attempted to apologize. "I'm sorry, lass. Keelin. I should no' have done tha'."

She stared at him, eyes raging like an ocean storm as they flicked over him, leaving his skin burning everywhere they touched. Her chest rose and fell rapidly. Her lips were red and swollen from his kisses. She took a step toward him.

Lucian held up a hand to stop her. "No, lass. Stay right where ye are."

Hurt darkened her eyes. "Lucian—"

But he wouldn't let her say what he knew she was going to say. "No, Keelin. Please," he added with a note of desperation. "I can no' do this."

They stared at each other a moment longer, and then she quickly skirted around him and headed toward the back of the house.

When she was gone, Lucian dropped into the nearest chair, his head in his hands. He could barely believe what had just happened.

What the bloody hell had just happened?

He sat up. He needed to leave. Get out of this house. Before he followed her back to that bedroom and finished what he'd started. Lucian stood so fast he knocked the chair over. Leaving it on the floor, he pulled the door open, locked the knob, and rushed outside, pulling it shut behind him. The next thing he knew, he was leaning against a tree trunk in the woods behind her house, staring at the light coming from her kitchen windows. The snow was falling harder now, and it gained a good inch before he finally saw the light go out.

He breathed in the frosty air, letting the chill cool his blood. He wasn't cold. Actually, the freezing wet air felt good against his overheated skin.

Gods, he'd been on the verge of shifting! Such was the wanting he felt for that woman. He'd never been that close to losing control. If he hadn't broken it off when he had...

No. He didn't even want to think it.

And he hadn't gotten any more information from her. Like why she wasn't surprised to be attacked by the crazy ones, or why she didn't seem exactly shocked that Cedric had sent him to watch her. No, he'd been too busy eating a good meal and feeling the needs of his cock.

It could not happen again. Cedric trusted him to do this.

And he would not fuck it up.

CHAPTER 7

Keelin lay in bed, but she wasn't the least bit sleepy. How could she be after what had just happened?

It was foolish of her to let him touch her like that. He was a werewolf. She didn't even know how sex worked with a werewolf. That was one topic her mom had never discussed with her.

He'd actually *growled,* for God's sake.

Chills chased each other across her skin remembering the sounds he'd made. Dangerous or not, there was nothing that turned on a woman more than hearing a big, strong man moaning—or growling as the case may be—in your ear. He hadn't left her because of a sudden attack of morals. She'd felt how he'd responded to her, and Lucian had been all in it. Just as she was. The only reason he'd pulled away was because he'd been on the brink of losing control. She'd seen his face. He hadn't tried to hide it. If she were to guess, Lucian had been minutes—if not seconds—away from shifting right there in her kitchen.

He could've killed her.

Keelin sighed and rolled over. On top of everything else was the guilt. She was wracked with it. It didn't matter that Brian was gone almost a year now. She felt dirty, as though she'd cheated on him, which she knew was ridiculous but was there all the same. She'd practically thrown herself at another male. And she'd done it in the house she and Brian had made into a home. *Their* home. The fact that Brian would want her to move on, and had told her as much in the letter he'd left her, didn't make it any easier.

Eventually, she must've fallen asleep, for the next time she opened her eyes her alarm was going off. Keelin got ready for work, her movements stiff and automatic from lying in the same position all night. Every time she passed a window, she peered through the blinds, looking for Lucian, but there was no sign of her wolf protector. Surely, he hadn't really slept outside in the snow all night. He would be frozen solid by now.

Then again, why the hell should she care? It's not like she wanted him around.

But the problem was, she did. And if she were going to be totally straight up with herself, it wasn't so bad having all that hotness around to look at. Lucian made her feel alive, really alive, for the first time since Brian's death.

However, he was also dangerous, and having him around put a major glitch in her life and did not help her remain under the radar. Keelin sighed as she pulled on her boots and zipped up her heavy coat. All she could hope for was that everything that had happened between them the previous evening had spooked him into tucking tail and running back home.

Unfortunately, she soon learned he wasn't scared off that easily. Throughout the day, as she trekked through the forest behind Eddie, she would catch glimpses of a large, red, wolf-like creature. Lucian watched her always, well within listening distance. At first, she was worried her boss would spot him. He didn't look like a normal wolf—he was larger, more muscular, and had less fur—but after a few hours, she realized she only saw Lucian because he wanted her to see him. For as large as he was, he moved through the trees with a stealth that wasn't natural, even for normal wolves, appearing in one place and then another faster than human eyes could track and as silent as a flake of snow. Whenever she happened to look up and see him, his gaze speared her with such heat she felt like she had embers beneath her clothes. It was spooky, like being haunted by an entity who seemed harmless but who might start throwing dishes around at any moment.

By the time she drove home, Keelin was in such a state of paranoia she would've sworn on her mother's grave he had somehow discerned everything there was to know about her just by watching her test the soil and plant a few trees. She kept glancing in her rearview mirror, expecting to find him sitting in her back seat, his gray eyes cold and full of accusations.

When she finally pulled into her driveway, Keelin's nerves had had about all they could take. She was ready for a hot meal and a quiet night.

Once inside, she went straight to the kitchen to put

her stuff down and turn on the teakettle. She didn't bother turning on any lights. She planned to get her tea, take a steaming hot shower, and crawl into bed to zone out on her latest Netflix binge. As she passed by the window, something caught her attention from the corner of her eye.

Squinting into the darkness, something moved, and a startled shriek shot from her throat before she could stop it. Keelin slapped her hand over her mouth to prevent more. The shadowy form of a very large man stood on her back porch. Heart pounding, Keelin sidestepped out of view. She took a few deep breaths, scolding herself for being so jumpy, then stepped back in front of the pane and stared at the male on her porch.

Lucian stood outside her back door, hand raised to knock. When he saw her through the glass, he slowly lowered his arm and waited silently for her to decide whether or not she was going to let him in.

After a quick debate between her head and her heart, she unlocked the door and gestured for him to come in. He was wearing only a black, long-sleeved pullover and jeans and boots. No coat. No hat. No gloves. "How are you not cold?" she blurted.

He cocked his head at her and narrowed his eyes, as if that was the very last thing he imagined would come out of her mouth. It took him a moment to answer her. "Wolves run hot."

She remembered the heat of his body when he'd held her the night before, and felt the blood rush to her cheeks. He wasn't lying. "What do you want, Lucian?"

He raised one eyebrow at her blunt tone. "I just wanted tae check on ye."

"There's no need," she told him. "I was just settling in for a night of binge watching whatever mindless series is popular on Netflix at the moment. Pretty boring."

Lucian leaned toward her, and Keelin raised her eyes to find his face inches from hers. Her breath caught, and her skin suddenly felt hot and entirely too sensitive beneath the layers of her clothes. His blue-gray eyes darkened to the steely color of storm clouds. "Ye are the furthest thing from 'boring' I've ever met, Keelin Doran."

Gods, he smelled good. Like fresh snow and pine and something distinctly male. Keelin stepped back.

"Why do ye always run from me, lass?"

She forced herself to meet his eyes. "I'm not running anywhere." Not yet. "I'm right here."

He grunted. "Yer running all the same."

The teakettle released a steamy whistle. Turning away, she flicked on a light before she turned off the burner, leaving the hot water on the stove. "Are you hungry? I was just going to have some tea, but I'm sure I could find you something." Yanking open the door to her freezer, she started pulling out frozen meat and fish and setting it on the counter. "Everything is frozen, but I could thaw it out for you."

"Do ye always use food tae avoid uncomfortable situations? If so, it's a fine defense mechanism ye have there. At least I will no' have tae worry about goin' hungry."

Keelin heard the slightest hint of humor in his voice. It was such a surprise, she froze for a second until the frozen fish she was holding began to hurt her hand from the cold.

She dropped it on the counter and turned to him with a frown. "Are you making fun of me?"

"Aye." His lips quirked.

She scowled at the food on the counter. He was right. She did use food to diffuse situations. A habit she'd gotten from her mother. Looking up at him, she asked, "So, are you hungry or not?"

"No, lass. But thank ye." Crossing his arms over his chest, he leaned back against the counter. Waiting for her next move.

He filled her small kitchen, and Keelin felt the walls closing in on her until she found it hard to breathe. Grabbing the frozen meat, she began to put it away again, just to have something to do. "You can't just follow me around all day, Lucian." She closed the door and turned to face him, hands on her hips. "I saw you today, sneaking around my worksite. What if Eddie had seen you? My boss," she clarified when he frowned in confusion.

"Yer boss will no' see me."

"But what if he did. How will I explain that? How will I explain *you*?"

"I told ye, ye will no' need tae *explain* me."

But she wasn't ready to give up that easily. "But you can't just be hanging around all the time—"

He shoved off the counter, appearing directly in front of her between one heartbeat and the next. "Aye," he growled. "I can. 'n' I will. Why the fook do ye think I'm here, Keelin?" He didn't give her a chance to answer. "I'm here tae protect ye. 'n' that's what I aim tae do."

"I thought you were here to keep an eye on me so I don't tell the world about you on the evening news."

"Aye. That tae."

"I still don't know what exactly I need protecting *from*," she said. "The other night was just a freak occurrence."

"I would like tae ken the answer tae that myself. But for now, I'm following the orders o' my alpha."

"Is that the only reason you're here?" She sucked in a breath and held it. Sure, the thought had been lingering, there on the edge of her tongue, but she couldn't believe she'd actually said it.

Reaching behind her head, Lucian pulled the elastic band from her hair, releasing it from its ponytail. "No." He picked up a lock of her hair and rubbed it between his fingers. His expression didn't change, except for his eyes. When he raised them, they were bright as they'd been the night before. "Yer locks are the softest thing I've ever felt." Bending down, he buried his face in the side of her neck and breathed in deep. "'n' ye smell sweet. So verra sweet." His mouth was pressed into a flat line when he straightened again. Suddenly, he dropped her hair, and his eyes bore into hers. Angry. Accusing.

Keelin released the breath she hadn't realized she'd been holding. She waited for the accusations. For the striking blow.

With a low snarl, he spun on his heel and slammed out her back door, leaving her cold and alone in her kitchen.

"Ye need tae find someone else tae watch the lass." Lucian pointed at Duncan, lounging on the couch "reading" the latest Sports Illustrated swimsuit edition. "Let him go prance around her. The eejit isnae doing anything else these days except being a nuisance." But as soon as he'd said it, the off chance that Duncan would succeed in using his charms to win over Keelin had him growling in disagreement of his own idea. "No. No' him." He looked around the room, his eyes lighting on Marc. "Him." He dropped his arm. "Or Brock. Fook it! I dinna care. Any wolf but me!"

Cedric tore his eyes from the chessboard laid out on the table in front of him and sighed loudly. "Brock is still spooked from his Fae adventures and will no' leave Heather's side for more time than it takes tae piss, ye ken that. And Marc is about tae take a trip tae Texas tae help Keegan with some Colorado pups who are no' in agreement with the change in leadership. So, unless yer good with Duncan—"

A growl ripped through the air. "No. No' Duncan. I dinna trust him."

"Then ye have tae watch the woman, Lucian. I need ye tae do this for me."

Lucian fell into the chair opposite Cedric and studied the board for a few seconds, his mind racing as he tried to think of another alternative. Picking up the queen, he moved the piece diagonally across the board. "Checkmate."

Leaning forward in his chair, Cedric studied the board for long seconds. With a scowl, he crossed his powerful arms over his wide chest and sat back with a huff. "Aye," he growled. Then he rubbed his eyes with his fingertips.

He looked tired. But lack of sleep was part of the gig of being the head of a pack of temperamental werewolves. And the threat of having a hoard of Dark Fae sickened with addiction released upon the world at any moment didn't help matters. Worrying about one human woman didn't make sense. "It's more than her knowledge o' us. Is it no'?"

Cedric stared at him steadily, his expression giving nothing away. "Why would ye say that?"

"Because I can think o' no other reason a human woman would need tae be watched so closely right now. Other humans ken about us. I dinna see anyone running their arses off tryin' tae keep a watch on all o' them."

"Other humans aren't Keelin."

Lucian leaned forward and braced his elbows on his

knees. "What does tha' *mean*, Cedric? I have a right tae ken, if I'm the wolf watching the lass."

"Dinna snarl at me, pup. I have enough on my mind withou' dealing with your crabbit arse."

Biting back the sharp retort that sprang to his tongue, Lucian forced himself to sit back in his chair. Marc got up and took his glass to the kitchen, giving Lucian a puzzled look on his way past, like he'd only just noticed he was there. "If yer done with me, I need tae get back tae Bronaugh. She's no' feeling like herself."

Cedric waved him away. "Och. Aye. Off with ye, then. Thank ye for the update, Marc. I'll call ye."

"Aye." With a nod at Duncan, who ignored him completely and only had eyes for the curvy blonde on the magazine cover, he was gone.

Lucian watched him go. Something was definitely up. Something no one was bothering to tell him about.

"What's going on with ye, Lucian? Why all the blathering about such a simple task? Ye never grumbled so much before. And that's sayin' a lot for ye."

He turned back to find Cedric's white-blue eyes burning a hole through him, and the excuse he'd been about to tell him sputtered and died on his lips. The pack master had an uncanny way of seeing right through his bullshit. It used to infuriate him. He'd felt like it was an intrusion on his private feelings. But now it was almost a relief to have someone willing to share the burden of the rollercoaster of emotions constantly pitching around inside of him. "I dinna ken."

Lacing his fingers over his stomach, Cedric studied

him much like he had the chessboard. "Have ye seen anything we need tae be worrying about?"

Lucian shook his head. "No. No' yet. But it's only been a couple o' days."

"Then what's eatin' at ye?"

He shrugged one shoulder. "Like I said, I dinna ken. I'm just…no' myself around the lass."

"Are ye scarin' her? I dinna want her scared. We'll never find out anything that way."

"No!" Lucian frowned. "At least no' on purpose."

"Ye mean tae tell me yer no' running around growlin' and barkin' at the poor woman fer lookin' at ye the wrong way?" The corners of his lips lifted in a smirk.

"No. I save tha' part o' my charming personality fer ye."

Though Lucian was perfectly serious, Cedric barked out a surprised laugh. "Aye, pup. That ye do." With a glance at Duncan, he lowered his voice. "So, go on then. Tell me what's eatin' at ye."

He shook his head. How to explain the aches and long-ings that flipped his stomach when he was anywhere near the lass? The way the hair rose on the back of his neck and his skin prickled when she was anywhere near him? And how he barely knew her but the thought of anyone harming so much as a strand of hair on her wee head sent him into a spiral of fury so hot he was surprised it didn't burn him alive—as he'd learned when her boss had spoken to her in a terse manner earlier in the day. "She…affects me."

"Affects ye how?"

"I dinna feel like myself around her. I feel…protective. Too protective." It was all he was willing to admit. No one else needed to know about the physical reaction to her. "And I dinna ken why. She is just a human."

"Like ye do with the pack?"

"No. No' like I do with ye. It's different."

A look of surprise passed over Cedric's face. "No shite?"

Getting more uncomfortable with this conversation by the second, Lucian shifted in his chair. "This is why one o' the others needs tae keep an eye on the lass."

"I do no' agree," Cedric told him, slapping his thigh in emphasis. "I think tha' is exactly the reason it *should* be ye."

Lucian opened his mouth to argue, even though he knew it would do no good, but he needed to try for his own peace of mind.

Before he could say anything, Cedric held up his hand, cutting him off. "Dinna try tae change my mind, Lucian. It will no' happen. Just keep an eye on the lass 'n' keep her safe from the soul suckers. Ye do no' need tae converse with her."

Lucian snapped his jaw closed. But then remembered something else he'd wanted to ask. "Dinna ye think there was something off about the night I found her?"

"What do ye mean?"

"Like, why was she wanderin' around in the woods in the rain? At night? In her nightclothes? Who does that? Except maybe for wolves like us? And maybe blood suckers? O' which she is neither."

"Cannae see Luukas or Nik wandering around in a nightshirt…Aiden, maybe…"

"That's no' my point."

Cedric focused on him again. "I dinna ken why females

do wha' they do. But that's one o' the reasons why I want tae keep an eye on her."

There was definitely something Cedric wasn't telling him.

"Keep a low profile," the pack master continued. "Dinna let her see ye hangin' around all the time, 'n' let the lass get comfortable. No' only will it give her a chance tae show her true colors, but it will flush out anyone else who is aimin' tae harm the lass if they think she's alone 'n' defenseless."

Lucian bared his teeth before he could stop himself. "That will no' happen."

"I'm countin' on it." Cedric grinned at him, then shooed Lucian away. "Now git on with yerself. The Prince has a tendency tae drop in any time he damn well feels like it these days, and ye dinna want tae get caught up in one o' his great ideas."

"Fook, no." Lucian jumped up from his chair. "I'm gonna go upstairs tae eat 'n' change, then I'll head back tae Keelin." He stopped. "Tae her house. The woods around her house. Not tae her. That is no' what I meant." Face burning, he walked quickly from the apartment, Cedric's laughter following him.

Ye gods, what the fookin' hell was wrong with him? At least Duncan had been too enthralled with the bare-skinned models on the pages to pay much attention to that conversation. It would've given him way too much ammunition.

Unlocking his door, Lucian felt a wave of relief as the cool silence of an empty apartment hit him. His unwanted houseguests were gone and he had the place all to himself again. Bronaugh's Aunt Nancy was a fine woman—for a Faerie—and she'd tried hard to stay out of the way, but she didn't put up with any "secrets" and even his most fearsome growls didn't scare her out of his business. So, though he would miss her cooking, he was glad she and her husband had moved down south to be closer to Bitsy and Keegan. It was good they were there. There was too much unrest with the southern wolves ever since the Texas pack master won a fight to the death and acquired the Colorado pack.

Lucian wasn't envious of the male. Keeping one pack under control was hard enough. Add in a bunch of new wolves, many of whom were not happy with the change in leadership, and who lived in an entirely different state… no, that wasn't something he would wish on anyone. Keegan had his paws full, that was for sure. And his head-strong mate was only part of the problem.

Keelin's face suddenly flashed through his head, and he frowned, not understanding the similarity. Keelin was nothing like Bitsy. She was sweet and kind.

And human.

But she had a fire underneath. He'd felt it when they'd kissed. A fire that was sure to burn him if he touched it again. Perhaps that's where the comparison came from. Another picture of her flashed through his thoughts. This one was of her face, too. But this time her lips were swollen from his kisses and her eyes were dark with all of the blues of a raging ocean.

Lucian's breath left him in a whoosh. Aye. The lass was a sight to see when she was burning for him. His hand drifted to the front of his jeans, cupping the bulge there that grew harder and more uncomfortable by the second. When he realized what he was doing, he curled his fingers into a fist. It would do no good to get himself all worked up. He would not be seeing her again. Not like that. He would keep his distance. Watch her from afar. Make sure no more soul suckers came around and that what had happened the other night was nothing but a freak thing. That's all. Keelin wasn't a target. Just a silly human wandering around in the woods when she should be warm and cozy in her bed.

He would prove it.

CHAPTER 9

Keelin woke with a scream trapped beneath the large hand covering her mouth.

"Shhhh. Dinna scream. It's me. Lucian. I'm no' here tae hurt ye, lass, but we have tae go."

Lucian. She would recognize that growling voice anywhere.

It had been almost three weeks since she'd last seen him. After the night of their *almost* second kiss, he'd stomped out her back door and out of her life. The next day, she'd had to work in the nursery, and was kind of relieved to have the alone time. She'd needed it to get her head together without him around to distract her. But even without being near him, the pull was too strong, and by the end of her shift, she'd come to a decision to stop feeling guilty about Brian. Brian was gone. Nothing she did or didn't do would bring him back. And she truly believed he wouldn't want her to spend the rest of her life alone, pining for a love that was lost.

However, finding new love with a werewolf wasn't something she was sure could happen. For many reasons. The least of which being the...physical aspects. So, she would just have to ask Lucian if a relationship—an intimate relationship—would be possible between them. Because if not, he really needed to stop almost kissing her.

She'd half-expected him to show up at her back door again that night, but he hadn't. And after a restless few hours, she'd eventually gone to bed. He didn't show up the next day or the next night. Or the one after that. And she knew this for sure because she might have gotten up one or five times to check outside. By the end of the week, she knew he wasn't coming back. Perhaps his alpha had changed his mind about the need to watch her. Perhaps Lucian was defying him by staying away. Perhaps he wanted nothing to do with this silly human woman. In any case, it was obvious he wasn't obsessing about her the way she was about him.

Or maybe she was completely wrong.

"We need tae go, Keelin. Now." The words were hissed into the darkness.

She nodded, and his hand left her mouth. It didn't occur to her to question him. She could sense his urgency.

Besides, she had a horrible feeling all of her questions would be answered within the next few minutes.

A second later, she heard drawers opening and closing. Something landed in her lap as she pushed herself up into a sitting position.

"Put those on." His voice was barely above a whisper. "It's snowing 'n' I canna have ye freezin' tae death before I can get ye warm again." Something else landed on the bed beside her. Then her closet door opened and closed and she heard the soft thud of her boots land beside her dangling feet.

She lifted the first item and discovered it was a pair of pants, the khaki all-weather kind she wore for work. Which was good, as she was sleeping in nothing but a short-sleeved nightshirt she'd picked up from Walmart that said, "wake free zone" across her chest. It barely covered her ass. As she turned the pants around, trying to feel which side was the front in the darkness of her room, they were taken from her hands.

"Right foot."

Keelin obediently lifted her foot and he slid a pant leg on, then repeated the process on the other side. Hands on his hard shoulders, she stood before him like a child as he yanked them up over her hips. For a brief second, she felt his warm breath on the bare skin of her belly before her shirt fell down to cover her again, and her groin muscles clenched with anticipation. She felt her neck and chest heat as the blood rushed close to the surface, and she was glad it was dark so he wouldn't see her reaction to him.

Nothing was said between them as he assisted her in pulling on her socks and then, finally, her boots. But she could swear she felt his hands tremble.

It didn't occur to her until much later that the reason he moved around so easily in the dark was because he could see a hell of a lot better than she could. A flaw in her makeup. Which meant it was very possible he'd seen a hell of a lot.

Her heart raced as she imagined all kinds or horrific

reasons he was getting her out of bed in the middle of the night. "Lucian—"

"Do ye trust me, Keelin?"

The world stilled around her as she searched for his face in the dark. Then he took her hand and led her from the bedroom without waiting for her to answer him.

But she did anyway. "Yes." Surprisingly, she wasn't lying.

Keelin didn't know if he'd heard her until they got to the back door. He didn't open it right away. Instead, he stopped and turned to face her.

The light was on over the stove. He must've turned it on when he came in. *When he broke in,* she corrected herself, trying to get a grip on the situation. In the faint glow, the planes and angles of his face were thrown into shadow. But his eyes burned bright. Storm clouds lit by the moon. They traveled over her face briefly before settling on her mouth.

"Do ye have a coat?"

She pointed toward the front of the house. "In the closet by the front door."

He left her briefly to go get it, and helped her put it on. "When we get outdoors, dinna look around. Dinna hesitate. Ye may hear things, things tha' are disturbing. Ignore it. We're going tae run tae the trees behind yer house. Run as fast as ye can 'n' dinna stop."

"What about you?"

He took her hand again. "I'll be right there with ye. I will no' let anything happen tae ye."

She'd known whatever was happening wasn't good. Fear made her tongue feel thick in her mouth, choking back the question spinning around in her head. But she needed to know. "Lucian, what are we running from?"

He studied her face. "I'll tell ye when I have ye somewhere safe."

Keelin took a deep, steadying breath and tightened her grip on his hand. Her heart felt like it was going to pound out of her chest. But that was good. It got the adrenaline going. She had a feeling she was going to need it.

"Keelin."

She looked up him, clenching her jaw to keep her teeth from chattering. And they hadn't even gone out into the cold yet.

"It will be okay. I promise ye tha'."

"You shouldn't make promises you can't keep."

"I never break a promise, lass." Then he kissed her hard on the mouth, and opened the door.

Snow was falling in thick, white flakes. It landed silently on the deck, covering the ice that had frozen over late in the night, deceiving her into thinking she would have some traction in the snow. Luckily, Lucian was prepared, and kept a firm grip on her elbow, holding her upright when she would've fallen on her ass. Keelin got her footing, and crunched across the deck. She tried to walk as quietly as she could, but her boots, though warm, weren't exactly stealthy.

Her wolf, on the other hand, was treading silently as a wraith in his thick-soled black hiking boots. Keelin wondered briefly how he was able to walk so quietly, but then they were down the steps and in her back yard.

Lucian paused, hugging the edge of the deck, keeping them hidden. Turning his head to the right and then the left, he peered into the darkness before setting his sights on the tree line about two hundred yards straight ahead. Keelin was grateful she'd never gotten around to putting up a fence. She liked having her yard open to the creatures of the forest. They were always welcome to pass through her land. Her neighbors weren't of the same mindset, if the boxed in back yards to either side were any indication.

A strong arm pulled her in close and Lucian bent down to whisper in her ear. "On the count o' three, I need ye tae run like your life depends on it. Straight into the trees. Dinna look around. Dinna stop fer anything. Understood?"

Keelin nodded.

Taking her hand again, Lucian squeezed it. Once. Twice. And on the third time, he ran, pulling her behind him.

As she ran, she listened. But she heard nothing in the silence of the snowfall other than her breathing and the thud of her feet as they landed in the accumulating snow. Though she was running with everything in her, Lucian could've been out for a nice evening jog. Every couple of seconds, he would glance around. And though he'd warned her not to, Keelin couldn't resist doing the same. The fact that clouds hid the moon and she couldn't even see the snowflakes landing wetly on her face didn't deter her. It was more a nervous reaction than anything else.

If it weren't for the tension she felt radiating from Lucian through the link of their connected hands, she would think this was nothing but a big joke. But, somehow, she knew it wasn't.

Lucian's fingers tightened on hers as his head suddenly

whipped to the left and he stared hard into the storm. Squinting against the fat wet flakes, she could barely see him lift his nose into the breeze, sniffing the air. He picked up his pace, forcing her to run faster, and when she couldn't keep up, he pivoted on his heel and caught her midsection with his shoulder, then hefted her up and kept running. He barely broke stride.

Keelin fisted the back of his flannel shift and hung on for dear life as she fought to catch her breath while hanging upside down. Her hair brushed his ankles, and she prayed it wouldn't tangle around his legs and rip from her head. Around her, the night erupted into sounds muffled by the snow—soft, yet thunderous, footfalls like a herd of elk she'd once startled when she left for work one morning. And a horrendous stench soured the back of her throat.

A vibration rumbled through the hard shoulder shoved into her gut, her wolf growling at the threat. She wondered why he hadn't shifted. Wouldn't he be able to fight better? Run faster? But the answer came to her almost immediately. He had stayed in his skin for her. He was trying to save her. But Keelin knew it was no use.

She knew what was coming for her. It was more of those things. They'd found her.

When pine needles brushed the backs of her legs and arms, she knew they'd hit the trees. Lucian dumped her into the snow on her ass and began ripping off his boots. "I'm sorry, lass. But I cannae see them." He tossed the boots in front of her. "Bring these, if ye would. I dinna have any extras."

Keelin got to her feet and picked up his boots. They

were nearly twice the size of her own. "Bring them where?"

But he was already falling to his hands and knees. The wet, sucking sound of muscle tearing from tendons and the hard pop of bones filled her ears, drowning out the noise of the rain and their pursuers. "Stay with me," he gritted out just before his jaw lengthened and sharp teeth shot down.

The clouds shifted and the glow of the moon lit the area. Keelin watched with a strange mixture of fascination and horror as his powerful body shifted and contorted in ways that shouldn't be possible. He looked at her once, gray eyes alight with pain and magic, but he turned away when he saw her watching.

The entire change took only a matter of seconds. When it was over, and she found herself staring eye to eye with the large wolf, Keelin searched his eyes for the man she knew. He was in there still. She could see him in the stormy depths.

His upper lip lifted, exposing long, sharp teeth in a wicked snarl. Thinking she had misinterpreted things, Keelin took a swift step back. The wolf leapt straight at her as the moon disappeared behind the clouds, and she screamed, throwing her hands up in a pathetic attempt to protect herself.

Lucian knocked her back into the snow as he passed. A second later, an ungodly noise pierced her eardrum. Keelin slapped her icy hands over her ears, looking around wildly, peering through the darkness. The wolf had his jaws clamped around a human-like figure, but she knew from the smell it was one of those things that had chased her the other night. Getting to her feet, she backed away just far enough to be out of the line of fire.

But her caution was unnecessary. A large shape on all fours came toward her. Brushing against her trembling form, he growled low in his throat and gently took her arm between his teeth and started walking fast.

"Okay, okay. I'm coming."

He dropped her arm and she followed him, teeth chattering, up the mountain. When she had a hard time, she tucked his boots under one arm and took a handful of fur to steady her footing. He glanced back at her, but otherwise didn't seem to mind. They stayed off the main trail, veering to the left and taking the incline on a diagonal. His large head swung back and forth, nose in the air. Every once in a while, he would abruptly change direction.

Keelin's thighs and calves were burning and she couldn't feel her fingers or her face, but she doggedly continued on. She wasn't some weak female. She would keep up if it killed her. And at this point, she was pretty much on autopilot.

After what felt like hours, Lucian stopped. Unable to halt her momentum in time, she stumbled into his side. Righting herself, she took the opportunity to adjust his boots under her arm and get a better grip on his fur. He stood stock still, but beneath her frozen fingers she could feel tremors sliding across the skin on his back.

Keelin clenched her teeth together in an effort to keep them from chattering. Shifting from one foot to the other, she stretched her tired muscles as best she could without losing her grip on Lucian, for the snow was coming down even harder now, making their trek more and more difficult. But, hopefully, it was also impeding the things they were trying to outrun.

He glanced back at her, tossed his head, and started moving again. This time, he headed straight up the mountain, picking up speed.

She jogged along beside him, her breath coming in short bursts. Keelin had never been so grateful for her extra strength and all of the exercise she got on an almost daily basis hiking these mountains on the job. But, even still, she knew she wasn't going to last much longer keeping this pace. Numb with cold, the rush of adrenaline that had been fueling her was wearing off, and she was crashing hard. But sheer stubbornness kept her putting one foot in front of the other. The wind burned her face, or maybe those were tears. From fear? From exhaustion? She couldn't have said.

Finally, Lucian slowed. Picking his way through the snow, he sniffed the air, his ears cocking this way and that. Seemingly satisfied, he nodded his big head at her and set off again.

Keelin was ready to bury herself in the snow and pray for a quick death when she saw it. Straight ahead. A wooden shack, or maybe a small cabin, hidden among the trees with the mountain looming over it. To anyone not paying attention, it would appear to be a part of the mountain.

This time, the tears were tears of relief.

CHAPTER 10

Lucian inhaled deeply, sorting out the scents blowing around him. Nothing but the clean scent of snow, pungent pine, and the musty fragrance of wet fur—his, and the other winter creatures rooting around for food before the snow buried it. Not a trace of the sour stench of decaying flesh. The soul suckers hadn't followed them.

His instincts had been correct, then. For weeks now, he'd been watching Keelin from a safe distance. Following her throughout the day while she worked, and camping out of doors within the trees behind her home come nightfall. Every couple of days, Duncan would relieve him for an hour or two so he could run home and shower and get some food, but he never stayed away for long. Cedric hadn't offered any other relief, but after much self-evaluation, Lucian was good with that. He preferred the isolation. And the more he learned about her, the less he wanted Duncan around her.

Still, more than once, he'd been high tempted to leave

his post and tell his alpha to fuck off. Though he did his best not to intrude on her privacy, but only to ensure her safety, he still felt a wee bit like a peepin' Tom. All this time and effort to watch a human woman.

Other times, he was convinced his time wasn't wasted. No. Quite the opposite. He needed to be there, because, eventually, more of those things would be back. If they'd sniffed her out once, it wouldn't take them long to find the other humans in the area. He'd felt it in his bones. And he'd been right.

What he hadn't guessed, and couldn't have known, was that they would be coming for Keelin, specifically.

The smell had hit him long before he'd heard them. From his viewpoint in the trees, Lucian had searched the area around him, but saw nothing. However, he didn't need to see them to know they were there. The wind changed direction and the scent had grown stronger. They were getting close. Too close.

That was when he'd heard it. Whispers in the dark. The Dark Fae were coming, and not just the infected ones who smelled like rot, but the ones who hadn't been fallen prey to the addiction.

And they were coming for his Keelin.

Without pause, Lucian had jumped to the ground and taken off at a dead run for Keelin's house, his only thought to get her out of there. If it had only been soul suckers wandering about, perhaps she would've been okay hidden behind the walls of her home, but having lucid Fae directing them changed everything. She couldn't hide in plain sight if they knew where to find her.

By the time he'd reached the back porch, he could hear

the shuffle of multiple pairs of feet plowing through the newly fallen snow. They were still about a mile or so away, but would be there soon enough.

It was a miracle he'd gotten her out in time. Other than the one straggler he'd quickly taken out, none had followed them. Luckily, Brock had told him of how they could disappear before his eyes, but couldn't hide from his wolf. So, though he'd hated to do it in front of her, Lucian had shifted. And lucky he was that he had, for the fucker had been poised to bite her when he'd knocked her out of the way.

Terror lit his blood at the memory. Lucian shook it off as the snow continued to fall around him. She was fine. They were both fine. The storm was a gift from the gods. Though it slowed their ascent up the mountain, it would do well to mask their scent.

Keelin's fingers clenched a handful of fur on his back. He had no idea what to do with her now that he was responsible for her. What he did know was she wasn't going to make it much farther. He was impressed she'd kept up as well as she had.

Without realizing he was doing it, he'd led her toward the abandoned hunting cabin he sometimes used when he was running this mountain. No one knew about it. Not even Brock or Cedric. It was his own private place, a sanctuary in the middle of nowhere, with only the animals for company. It had four walls, a wood stove that doubled as a cooktop and a source of heat, and a simple bathroom built off the back for privy needs. Simple enough, and all he needed to spend a quiet night or two.

Now, as he led her forward to the isolated cabin, he

was second-guessing his decision. The door wasn't locked. Lucian kept it that way on purpose, in case some other overwhelmed soul needed a place to take shelter. He didn't worry about being intruded upon. There was no way anyone or anything would take a werewolf by surprise. He would hear and smell them long before they got anywhere near the place.

When Keelin saw where they were headed, she finally released the death grip on his fur and climbed the two steps onto the small porch. Lucian nudged her hand toward the door handle with his nose. With fingers stiff from the cold, it took her a minute, but she eventually got the door open. It swung inward, and she glanced back at him, her expression unsure.

Her cheeks were red from the wind, and her lips were blue with cold. Lucian snuffed in encouragement, and tossed his head toward the doorway, urging her to get in out of the weather. Once she was inside, he put his nose to the ground and did a quick perimeter check before he shifted back to his human form.

Without his fur to warm him, he shivered in a blast of icy wind. The snow was still falling in heavy, fat flakes. That was verra good. With any luck, after not finding Keelin in her home, the Fae would disperse back to wherever the hell they'd come from. He and Keelin could take shelter here for the rest of the night, and then he would figure out what the hell to do with her.

Satisfied they were as safe as they could be for the night, he let himself in to find Keelin standing just inside, stiff as the boards around her. Thinking he'd somehow missed something, he scanned the room, but found nothing for her to be frightened of. The place was just as he'd left it, swept clean of any little visitors, with spare clothes folded neatly near the "bed"—two open sleeping bags on an old mattress left there by the previous owner. There was even some water and half a box of crackers he'd left there a few nights before.

"L-L-Lucian?" Her teeth chattered loudly before she clamped her jaw shut.

Belatedly, he realized then how dark it must be for her. "Aye. It's me, lass."

"What is th-this place?"

"An old hunting shack. Abandoned. I use it sometimes when I'm in the area. We should be safe for the time bein'."

His boots fell to the wooden floor with a thud as she dropped them. Something tickled his nose—the scent of brine. Wondering how the salt of the great sea was traveling this far, even with the storm, Lucian frowned. But then he heard her sniffle, and he realized she was crying. "Och, lass. Dinna weep. It will all be okay. I promise ye tha'."

"I'm s-sorry. I'm just feeling a little overwhelmed. And tired. And so c-cold."

He stood awkwardly, trying to think of something to say that would ease her discomfort. "Being jarred from a restful sleep 'n' dragged out in tae the snow would be enough tae make anyone a wee bit emotional." He cleared his throat. "Thank ye for bringing me boots. My toes would freeze right off come tomorrow if ye hadn't, 'n' I'm quite attached tae them."

"The boots or the toes?" She sniffed.

Lucian grinned. "Both."

"Are there lights in here?"

"Aye, but I can no' light them or start a fire. I'm sorry, lass. The soul suckers will see the light 'n' smell the wood burning from miles away 'n' find us for sure."

"Thank you," she whispered fast and hard. "For coming to get me."

Lucian shifted his weight. Her vulnerability pulled on things deep inside of him. Things he hadn't realized were still there to yank on. "I have sleeping bags on the bed. We'll get ye warmed up straight away. 'n' dinna worry about no' being able tae see. I can see just fine for the both o' us."

She turned her head to look at him, and he felt the skin of his bare chest heat as though she were caressing him with her eyes. But that was foolish. She was human. She didn't have the night vision, no matter how it might seem so.

His voice, when he spoke, was rough with desire. "We'll stay here for the night, 'n' I'll figure out wha' tae do in the morning."

Her eyes flew to the general area of his face and she took a step away. But not far. Lucian felt the loss of her withdrawal, but it was short lived, for almost immediately, the scent of her rising desire rose in the air between them.

He felt himself thicken in response beneath his cupped hands as he quickly covered the growing proof of his weakness for her.

A clatter broke the silence, distracting him, like someone was playing Spanish castanets. He immediately tensed and cocked his head to listen, but it was only Keel-in's teeth chattering. He kept forgetting that unlike himself, who ran hot and was fine once he was out of the wind, even in his skin, she must be freezing. And as a human, she was much more fragile than he was. He needed to warm her up, or there would be consequences he really didn't want to be dealing with right now.

"Come, Keelin. Get into the sleeping bag and I'll get you something to drink." Taking her hand, which felt like ice, he said as he led her toward the bed, "Ye can trust me, lass. I hope ye ken that."

She didn't agree or disagree, but followed him without resisting.

He straightened the sleeping bags, one on top of the other, and got her snuggled inside before he slipped on his spare pair of jeans, leaving them open over his stubborn erection as she couldn't see well enough to notice, and padded barefoot to the little kitchen setup to get her a bottle of water. Before returning to the bed, he cracked the door and listened for any signs of the Faeries, sniffing the air until he was satisfied they still hadn't been followed. He closed the door, sliding the lock home. Then he checked the locks on the windows.

Her muffled voice came from the direction of the bed. "Are you sure about th-th-that fire?"

Turning away from the window, he approached Keelin and sat down gingerly on the end of the mattress. "Aye, lass. I apologize. I should have brought ye something warmer tae wear."

"Please, don't apologize. I'm alive and safe because of you."

Her words warmed him deep inside. "Let's try tae keep ye tha' way," he told her gruffly.

They sat quietly for a bit after that, with only the chattering of her teeth breaking the silence. He was about to check the windows again when she asked, "So, why do you hate them so much? The Fae?"

Lucian rubbed his palms on his thighs. He didn't want to talk about such unpleasant things right now. "How do ye ken I hate them?"

She pulled the top sleeping bag higher around her chin. "I can tell by the way you talk about them. I can hear it in your tone."

Och, was he that transparent? "Faeries killed my family when I was just a pup. My friend 'n' I were playing down by the loch, 'n' when the sun set and we went back tae our village, our entire pack was dead. Including my maw, my da, 'n' my sister."

Sorrow weighed on him, suffocating him until every breath became a chore. It always came before the anger. But this time it felt different. Heavier. And Lucian realized Keelin was mourning with him.

"I'm so sorry," she told him, and he knew she meant it sincerely. "You were very lucky you weren't there."

"I was only a wee lad. Hadn't even gone through my first change, yet."

"Then why do you blame yourself for what happened?"

Lucian stiffened and shot her a look. "Wha' makes ye think I blame myself?"

"That's why you're so angry, isn't it? And why you're so merciless when it comes to those kind."

He waited for the anger she spoke of to chase away the sorrow as it always did, but this time it was suspiciously absent. "They dinna deserve mercy."

Keelin sat up, and one hand poked out of the blanket, searching for him.

He captured it within his own, and felt her squeeze his fingers. Warmth ran up his arm, and he laced his fingers through hers. He stared at their entwined hands with a mild sense of wonder and not a wee bit of confusion.

"You can't punish them all for something only a few did. And you can't punish yourself for being incapable of doing anything to stop it. Even if you'd been there, Lucian, even if you'd tried to fight back, there's nothing you would've been able to do. You have to stop punishing yourself for still being alive."

Her words resonated inside of him. Is that what he'd been doing all his life? Punishing himself? Punishing Brock? Punishing innocents?

A sneer lifted his upper lip. Faeries weren't innocent. Not by any means. But his Keelin was showing her true heart by trying to defend them, and he couldn't be angry with her for it. She didn't know the horror and havoc they caused.

The bed shook beneath his arse from her shivers, and they only got stronger over time. When he could take it no longer, Lucian stood up. "Scoot yerself over, Keelin."

"Wh-why?"

"Because I'm getting' in with ye before ye alert the soul suckers with all tha' clatterin'."

"S-sorry. It's just so cold in here."

"Aye. Move over, lass. If ye freeze on my watch, Cedric will no' ever let me forget it."

He thought she was going to protest again, but after a few more rounds of shivering and chattering, she scooted closer to the wall. Remembering she still wore her boots and having no desire to get his shins all bruised up, Lucian reached under the sleeping bag and pulled them off. He set them near the end of the bed by his own and crawled beneath the flannel with her. "Roll over," he told her. The words came out as little more than a growl.

She obediently turned until she faced the wall.

Lucian slid an arm under her neck and pulled her into his body, suppressing a groan when the softness of her arse curved perfectly into his hardness. The pants she wore were thin, and only partially covered by her jacket. She trembled against him, and he gritted his teeth as he tightened his other arm around her. "Ye should take off yer coat."

"That kind of d-defeats the purpose, d-doesn't it?" she said between chatters. "I've always been t-told to wear l-layers."

"Och, no. Tae many clothes keep ye from the warmth o' another body. 'n' I didn't exactly give ye time tae layer up now, did I?"

Keelin was silent for a bit. "N-no," she finally said. "You really d-didn't. But I'll forgive you because of c-circumstances and all."

He helped her pull her coat off, and laid it over her on top of the sleeping bag. Then he pulled her close again. Her shirt was even thinner than her pants. It was no wonder she was so cold. Lucian silently chided himself. He should've taken the extra few seconds to find her a heavier shirt. It wouldn't have made that much difference in the grand scheme of things.

But it wasn't the delay it would have caused that had

him turning his thoughts away from finding something long-sleeved. It was guessing what he now knew to be a fact.

She wore nothing beneath the one she had on. And if she'd been made to change shirts...

Lucian's fingers gripped the loose material over her soft stomach as he buried his face into the soft strands of her long locks. The clean scent of her shampoo filled his nose, only slightly overpowering the warm honey flower scent of her skin. The instinct to press his rapidly growing erection into the soft flesh of her arse hit him hard, but he had no right. She was not his. And he had no wish for a female of his own. This physical attraction was nothing but a weakness.

But even worse than his need to sink into the heat of her body, was the need to be always near her person. Even if he couldn't touch her at all. Keelin emitted a calm energy he found...peaceful. A rare experience. And when he wasn't with her, he found himself craving that energy. He could breathe around her.

His Keelin was smart. And brave. And warm. And caring about others beside herself. A rare find, indeed. He didn't need to know her long to know this about her. The purity of her soul shone brighter than the sun. It was in everything she said and everything she did. And this...*this* was the real reason he resisted the lure of her company, if he were to be honest. Lucian was drawn to her light like a fallen angel craved the embrace of a heaven he no longer deserved. Her goodness exposed all of his faults. The violence with which he lived his life. The anger. The hatred.

He did not deserve to be with a lass such as Keelin.

The soft skin of her palm slid over the back of his hand, holding his hand to her belly and disrupting his thoughts, and he noticed her shivering had stopped. Grinding his jaw against the regret, he started to roll away to give her some space.

But Keelin only tightened her grip on his hand, and pulled his arm closer around her, until his fingers brushed the full under curve of her breast.

Lucian shut his eyes tight, and tried not to move. He tried hard. But it seemed his hand was not attached to the rest of his body, for with a will all their own, his fingertips tentatively traced that curve.

Keelin's breath caught, then rushed out on a shaky exhale. But she did not remove his hand.

Lucian could not breathe at all. That barest of touches had left him shaken to the darkest hollows of his core.

"Lucian?" she whispered.

He grunted something along the line of "Aye?" at her in response.

"Can someone like you and someone like me…is it possible for us to be…intimate?"

Lucian realized at that moment he'd been wrong. The lass was no angel. She was the devil herself. Here to tempt him from all of his good intentions. How could he answer such a question, when he knew where it would lead?

Keelin twisted her head and her upper body toward him. His senses went into overload as the softness of her breast filled his palm and silky strands of her hair slid across his jaw.

Gods, she smelled good. Felt even better.

"Lucian?"

A million different responses ran through his head. Responses he *should* give her. Responses that would shut this conversation down tight, never to be opened again. But in the end, he couldn't bring himself to lie to her. "Aye," he said after a pause. "It's verra possible." He would have to be careful not to hurt her. Stay in control of his strength. But…aye. It was possible, and a common occurrence with some wolves.

"Then why do you run from me?" She threw his own words back in his face. When he didn't answer her right away, she released his hand and turned back toward the wall, and the steel rod of her spine was as good as a wall between them. "Never mind…you don't need to say it out loud…just forget I said anything…with everything that's going on, my imagination is probably getting the better of me and I'm seeing signs that aren't really there…it's rather embarrassing, actually…just, please, forget I said anything."

She said all of that in one long, continuous sentence. And when she finally stumbled to a stop long enough to take a breath, something akin to anger loosened his jaw. "What fool thing is this going through yer head, Keelin?"

"It's okay, Lucian. Truly," she said to the wall. "I know I'm not very pretty. Not that I'm ugly, either. But I'm just…I don't know…average. And a guy like you—with that face and that body and that accent and all—you probably have women falling at your feet all the time." She took a deep breath. "I should just shut up now."

Though his chest swelled from the compliments, he was flabbergasted by the rest of the words coming out of her mouth. So much so, he could think of nothing to say that would convey to her how absolutely wrong she was. Lifting himself up onto one elbow, he stared down at the woman, wondering how in the world someone so smart could be so utterly daft. "Ye believe...ye cannae possibly think..." Lucian took her gently by the shoulder and rolled her stiff body toward him until she was on her back. Brushing her hair away from her face, he memorized every freckle on her wee nose. "Keelin, that's no' the case at all."

Her eyes searched him out in the dark, but she quickly looked away. He thought perhaps he'd seen the sheen of tears, but her voice was steady when she said, "I'm trying to be mature about all of this. Really, I am. So, please don't be afraid to be honest with me, Lucian. I'm a big girl. I can take it."

"Why dinna ye start with being honest with *me*," he told her.

Her eyes flew back to his face, and with her next words, he was caught in the turbulent hues of the sea, rising higher and higher to crest upon the tip of the waves. Soul suckers could be pounding down the door and he wouldn't be able to look away from those eyes. "I am being honest with you," she said. "I know we don't know each other very well, but I'm...drawn to you. Physically, and otherwise. I don't know what or why or how. But there it is. At first I thought I was just lonely." She paused. Took a deep breath. "Then you disappeared from my life, and yet you were still there, everywhere I turned. Not Brian. *You.* And I would not be lying if I said I would be totally okay with exploring that attraction. Right now."

Though her face reddened with an innocence belying her words, her body emitted a scent so sensual Lucian couldn't stop the deep growling purr that rumbled in his throat. At the sound, her eyelids dropped and her lips parted, that heavenly scent rising up even stronger between them, and before he knew himself what he was about, Lucian lowered his head and touched his lips to hers.

Sweet.

So sweet.

He thought he was better prepared this time. Thought he could control the beast within him that wanted to take her like the animal he was. He had expended a lot of energy shifting not an hour before, and even had the satisfaction of a kill. Normally he would be calm and sated for hours afterward. But not this time. Not with this woman beneath him. Not with her opening her sweet mouth to deepen the kiss. Pressing her soft curves into the hard planes of his chest and stomach. Wrapping her arms around his neck to pull him closer when she couldn't reach him.

The thin cotton of her shirt was as if there were nothing between them. And yet, at the same time, it felt like a barrier of armor. With a growl, Lucian yanked it up as high as he could without breaking the kiss that felt as necessary as breathing to him.

Keelin arched her back off the mattress, pressing her breasts against his chest. Then reached behind her head, grabbed the neckline, and pulled the offending garment off, breaking their kiss only for the brief moment it took to separate it from her completely.

As soon as it was gone, Lucian wrapped his arms around her and rolled, pulling her on top of him. He wanted to see her. He needed to see her. Straddling her legs over his hips, he sat her up above him.

For all that was holy. He was *not* prepared.

CHAPTER 11

At first, Keelin thought something was wrong. She didn't know why else Lucian would be pushing her away. "Lucian? What is it? What's wrong?"

Her eyes had adjusted to the dark enough to see the shadow of his arm as he lifted his hand toward her. His warm palm cupped her breast, hefting the weight of it for a moment before his other hand did the same to the other side. Keelin arched her spine, her eyes fluttering closed as her head rolled back on her neck. The hard outline of his erection pressed against her core and she fought the urge to roll her hips.

She wasn't cold anymore.

"Gods. Ye fit perfectly in my hands. Like ye were made for me," he whispered beneath her. "So soft. 'n' kissed by angels."

Before she could ask him what that meant, he rose up from the bed and took her nipple in his mouth. Keelin cried out when she felt the wet heat of his tongue circle the tight bud.

"Shhhh," he whispered against her skin.

At this moment, she despised the darkness that kept her from seeing him as well as he could see her. Keelin's breath came hard as he teased her sensitive breasts, and though she tried to stay still and quiet, it was completely impossible. Her body took over, moans rising from her throat as her hips moving back and forth over the hard ridge between her thighs, seeking more of the feeling he was invoking. Brian flashed through her mind briefly, but Keelin firmly pushed him away. She didn't want her dead boyfriend anywhere in this bed. And she had no reason to feel guilty.

To her surprise, there was no guilt, only a swift surge of sadness. Like a breeze passing through. There and gone before it could really take hold.

Lucian took her nipple between his teeth and gently nipped the sensitive bud. Keelin jerked as a shock of desire stabbed through her from her breast to her loins. She managed not to make any noise this time, but shamelessly pushed her breast into his mouth for more. Her fingers tangled in his soft hair, holding his mouth to her, telling him what she wanted without words.

Yes. It was time for her to live again. And she wanted to feel alive. Really alive. Even if it was only for this brief time. Keelin hadn't realized until now just how checked out she'd been until this male had come into her life and awoken her senses with a jolt.

Warm lips left her breasts and began to work their way down her stomach. He pulled her forward, moving lower and lower until she was curled over him, knees on either side of his ribs and hands bracing her weight on either side of his head. Lucian's growl of displeasure when he reached the waistline of her pants sent chills skittering across her skin. Not from fear. More from anticipation of what he would do about the obstacle he'd encountered. She wished he'd rip them from her body, snow and cold be damned.

Keelin didn't have to wait long. Before she realized what was happening, he'd flipped her onto her back and his hands were on the waistband of her pants. Her breath caught and her heart stuttered in her chest as nerves finally caught up with her. She was not what one would call fashionably thin. Never had been. And though she was quite proud of her breasts—they weren't droopy and oversized in spite of her pudginess, and had quite a nice shape to them, in her opinion—she'd always been more self-conscious of the pooch of her belly and the flabbiness of her inner thighs. Would it turn him off?

Then again, would he even notice all that much? It was *very* dark, after all.

Lucian's hands stilled with her pants halfway undone, and Keelin felt her heart drop with disappointment.

His heated breath fanned the skin of her lower stomach. "I want tae see all o' ye, Keelin. May I do tha'?"

Her heavy heart came back to life with a rapid staccato of beats. "Yes."

His hands shook as he unzipped her fly. As she waited, barely breathing, he slid his fingers beneath the waistband. Taking his time, he pulled them off slowly, like he was savoring every inch of skin as it was revealed to him.

He paused with her pants around her knees. "Och," he breathed. "Yer even more bonny down here."

As he rid her of each pant leg, Keelin pressed her thighs together and reached for the blanket to cover herself. But he stopped her with a hand on her arm.

"No, lass. I beg ye. Dinna cover yerself 'n' deny me from this sight. I swear I would die from the disappointment."

He sounded completely serious. "Can you see me? Really see me?" As soon as the question was out of her mouth, she wished she hadn't asked.

"Aye, verra well. 'n' I've never been so glad tae have such good eyesight." To prove he meant every word, he reached out a trembling hand and ran his warm palm softly over the curve of her hip to her outer thigh. "Yer perfect, Keelin. I dinna want tae stop looking at ye." His thumb skimmed over the curls between her thighs.

Once.

Twice.

And again.

Blood rushed to the place he teased, pulses of desire heating her from the inside out as he brushed his thumb back and forth. Barely touching her. Keelin raised her hips, pressing herself against his finger as she sought a firmer touch. But he kept his thumb exactly where it was, denying her.

"Spread yer legs, Keelin," he ordered. "Let me see all o' ye."

Riding the waves of rising pressure deep in her belly, she did as he asked, spreading her legs. She inhaled sharply as the cold air touched her more intimately than his thumb.

He sat there on the side of the bed, saying nothing, but each breath was a sharp exhale. And though she couldn't see him as well as he could her, she could feel the smolder of his stare.

When he touched her again, his thumb slipping between the folds of her sex, she moaned, on the very edge of an orgasm. Keelin turned her head to the side, one hand covering her mouth to muffle the cry she couldn't hold back. She'd never felt so completely exposed in front of anyone before, both physically and emotionally, and it was the most erotic thing she'd ever experienced.

"Yer so soft, Keelin. So wet. I want tae be inside o' ye more than I ever wanted a lass in my life." He stroked her again, and she rocked her hips into his touch. "Gods, I'm no' gonna last long enough tae get inside." His thumb found her entrance and slipped inside, and she felt her sheath tighten. With a low growl, he returned to the sensitive bundle of nerves where everything centered. She started to tremble as she strained toward that elusive climax that was just beyond her reach.

"That's it, lass. I want tae see ye. Come for me, Keelin."

As soon as he said the words, her body obeyed his command. Keelin couldn't stop it, even if she'd wanted to. The pressure in her belly intensified to a peak of unbelievable pleasure before breaking her into a million pieces before bringing her crashing back down in wave after wave of shuddering release.

* * *

LUCIAN WATCHED her come for him, and he was ever so glad of the moonless night that prevented her from seeing him. For he feared she would scream for a completely different reason if she saw how close the beast within him was to the surface.

He wanted to be inside of her. Ached to feel her body tighten around him. Och. He wanted it so badly he was in a right state of agony. But he didn't trust himself to keep it together.

Lucian didn't know what it was about this particular lass. He'd been with many females in his life, human women included. As volatile as his wolf was, never before had he had this kind of trouble controlling his shifting nature while with one of them. Never like this. He could barely *kiss* Keelin without rousing the beast.

The scent of her sex strengthened with her release and filled the air with a scent so sweet he wished he could cover his entire body with it. Growling deep in his throat and unable to resist, he lifted her hips and covered her with his mouth. This time he didn't tease her, and his fingers dug into her hips when she began to convulse for the second time. Lucian opened his eyes and very nearly came himself as he watched her. Her chest and stomach were flushed with heat, breasts jostling with every jolt of her body, nipples hard and erect, head thrown back, hand over her mouth to muffle her cries.

Och. He couldn't wait to do this somewhere where he could hear every moan.

Except that wasn't going to happen. After this night, he would get Keelin somewhere safe, and then he was turning her safety over to Cedric and bowing out. Because if he stayed, he would begin to care. And the ones he cared about got hurt...or worse.

When her legs fell boneless to either side of his shoulders and her chest heaved as she caught her breath, Lucian took one last taste, enjoying the shiver that ran through her, and lowered her to the bed. He ran his hands down the skin of her inner thighs, so soft beneath his rough palms. Her sex was swollen and wet with his kisses.

He moaned aloud at the sight.

She reached for him, her voice low and husky and full of sex. "Lucian, come here."

She was inviting him to take what he needed, but he should not. He could not. Silently, he shook his head, even as the wolf inside of him howled with anticipation. Then, remembering she couldn't see him, he said, "I can no', Keelin."

With a frown, she sat up and reached for him again, this time finding his upper arms. She pulled him toward her. "Lucian, please. It's okay."

Carefully removing her hands, he ignored the way his skin burned with the need for her to touch him everywhere. "I can no'."

"You don't want to?"

"Och. Aye! O' course, I want tae. But I can no'."

"I don't understand. Did I do something?"

Aye, lass. Ye did. Ye were born with that hair and those eyes and that mouth and this body. 'n' your scent...gods, your scent. It's enough tae drive a male mad with lust. 'n' tae make it all worse, ye have a good heart, and yer tae smart for yer own good. 'n' ye make me feel things. Ye make me feel things. Things I have no right tae feel.

But all he said was, "No, Keelin. No. Ye are…perfect."

"Then, why aren't you…taking care of you? It's okay. I want you to do it." She gave a breathless laugh. "I *really* want you to."

Lucian stared into the ocean of her eyes, glowing in the aftermath of her pleasure, and took stock of what was going on inside of him, praying to the gods the break for conversation had calmed things down a wee bit. But, och, no. His muscles still ached from holding himself in such rigid control. His zipper bit into his swollen cock. And his wolf was right there, beneath the skin, tracking every tiny sound and movement she made, biding its time until the opportunity arose when it could pounce. Even if the wolf didn't hurt her, shifting with her beneath him—or closer —would.

He could not risk it.

"I'm sorry, Keelin." Frozen to the spot, he couldn't move. Not toward her, or off the bed. Perhaps honesty would be best. He didn't want to scare her, but she needed to understand the gravity of the situation. "It's no' tha' I dinna want tae. I do. Ye have no idea how much I do. But I…I'm no' feeling very in control o' my nature right now. And I can *no'* hurt ye. I would never forgive myself."

"Like that night at my house. When you ran away."

"Aye. Exactly like that night."

She was silent for a long moment, and he fought the drowning waves of disappointment that she'd given up so easily. *Och.* That was a ridiculous way to feel. She was taking his warning seriously, which was what she should do. What she needed to do.

"I trust you, Lucian."

His chest swelled with pride. An emotion he hadn't felt in a long time, at least not pertaining to himself.

"I know you won't hurt me. I trust you. Even if you don't trust yourself." With that decided, she rose up on her knees and came toward him.

Lucian watched her come, his arse rooted to the bed. She reached for him blindly, and even when one hand found his bare shoulder and the other the side of his face, he couldn't move. "Keelin!" The word was urgent. A plea for her to do what needed to be done, for he found he could not. Although he was no longer sure what exactly that meant. His fingers crushed the sleeping bag beneath him, gathering it within his fists and hanging on tight as she scooted closer until her knees touched his and her breasts swayed in his face.

Eyeing the mounds of flesh, he was beginning to understand the bloodsuckers need to bite, because his upper lip was pulled back from his teeth, his canines aching with the need to grow, to bite, to taste her flesh. A dangerous sound filled the cabin, and he realized it was coming from him.

It did not frighten her. No. Not at all. His nostrils flared as her scent surged. And then she was kissing him, her hands skimming his shoulders and chest, stopping here and there to knead the muscle. Lucian rose up onto his knees, planning to back away, even as he moaned at the feel of her touch. Touching him everywhere.

Touching him…there.

His hips jerked forward, pressing his erection into her palm.

Keelin curled her fingers around his balls and rubbed the heel of her hand up and down his length.

Lucian's eyes rolled back in his head. Breaking off the kiss, he kept his fists clenched at his sides as she rubbed him in all the right ways. He felt her lips at his throat, her warm tongue tasting him much as he had her. Distracted as he was, he didn't think about what she was doing until his erection sprung free from the hell of his jeans and her hand wrapped around his girth, skin to skin.

The beast took control. Flipping her over onto her hands and knees, he grabbed her hips and pulled her lovely arse up into the air, lining himself up at her entrance. He glanced up at her once, and saw she had braced herself, her long hair cascading over her back and shoulders to fall to either side.

With one powerful thrust, he buried himself balls deep inside of her. Lucian froze, completely undone by the feel of her body hugging him tight, even after all the pleasure he'd given her. He waited for his heart to slow, for the beast to get under control. "I'm sorry, lass. Keelin. I'm sorry…"

In response, she pushed her hips back and moaned.

He answered with a moan of his own. "Och. Yer gonna be the death o' me, lass." With a roll of his hips, he withdrew just a little and pressed back inside.

"Lucian, please," she moaned. "Fuck me."

Whether it was the raw need or the shock of those words leaving her sweet mouth, her words broke him from his stupor. Taking a good hold of her hips, he began a hard and fast rhythm, the beast growling with every thrust. His Keelin answered his need, meeting him stroke for stroke.

Way too soon, he felt his own orgasm come out of nowhere. He wanted to wait, to hold back, but it was all he could do to keep his wolf in check. There was no way he could control the pounding of his blood and the needs of his sex.

Lucian ground his jaw together as his balls tightened and raw heat shot up his spine and through his cock, but it wasn't enough to contain the deep growls of pleasure that burst from his throat. He emptied himself inside of her, and it was the best fucking release of his life.

It was only when it was over, and he'd thrust deep inside of her one last time before his muscles gave out and he collapsed over her limp form, that he realized she hadn't joined him.

Closing his eyes, Lucian rolled away and onto his back, leaving her on the edge of the bed. To stay or leave as she saw fit. He was disgusted with himself. Even in this… this…momentous occasion, he couldn't do anything right. "I'm sorry, Keelin," he said again, his throat thick with shame for getting too caught up in himself and failing her.

But it was better she knew what she was getting into. For this was only a prelude for things to come if she stuck around with him.

CHAPTER 12

Sara leaped over a puddle and quickly ducked inside the stone cottage. Shaking off the rain, she made her way over to the fire. It did little to ward off the chill, and for the seven hundredth and fortieth time that morning, she wished Thomas would pull his head out of the past and let them build houses just a wee bit more modern. With central heat and air. But the pack master was Scottish born and bred back in the day when "things were simpler", and he held true that it was still the way to live.

Personally, Sara didn't see how being warm and dry would hurt their quality of life. Her home was otherwise quite simple. Handmade furniture. Nothing fancy in her kitchen like a dishwasher or a microwave. But she'd had no luck convincing him otherwise. Hell, she was lucky they were allowed to wear something other than pants and dresses made from the hides of their kills.

The door opened again and Thomas came in, shaking

the rain from his long, dark hair like a dog. "Where is Finn?"

"I left him with Jaime. Ye said ye wanted a private meeting, and I figured tha' meant no wee ears listening."

"Aye. Tha' would be best." He joined her at the fire and stared into the flames, brows low over his amber eyes.

When time passed and he gave no indication of filling her in on what was going on, Sara turned to face him. "So, wha' is this all about?"

He held his hands out over the flames, much as she had just moments before, and glanced at her out of the corner of his eye. "Nothin' like the warmth o' a good fire on a dreary day."

Every day is dreary around here, no matter what the weather is like outside. But what am I tae do about it? "Thomas? Ye said ye had something o' importance ye wanted tae speak with me about," she prodded.

He glanced at her again, then with a sigh, he turned completely around. "Let's sit down." He indicated the small kitchen table behind her.

Unease slithered down her back and settled at the base of her spine. Thomas wasn't one to beat around the bush, and the fact he was doing so now made her nervous. She pulled out a chair and sat, waiting for him to do the same. She didn't offer him a cup of tea or a bite to eat. This was not a social visit.

"I need ye tae do something for me, Sara. Something I ken yer going tae balk about, but I need it from ye nonetheless." As he spoke, his voice vibrated with the timbre of the alpha.

Sara felt the pressure of his will, and fought against it. "What is it exactly yer asking me tae do?"

Leaning forward, he rested his large forearms on the table. Thomas was a large male, and he dwarfed her tiny round table that had always seemed plenty big enough for her and Finn. "How did ye feel about seeing Lucian again?"

Lucian? "That was months ago. Why are ye asking me about it now?" Actually, it had been almost a year since the Faerie prince had whisked them across the ocean and into the small kitchen of the house in Seattle. Sara had been shocked to see Lucian. But she'd been even more shocked to see Brock. She'd thought for sure he was dead. A wolf without its pack never lasted long, and she knew from Thomas he'd never fought his way into another after he'd been banished.

For something he'd never done. To protect his best friend.

Sara had thought she was in love with Lucian at the time. She was ready to leave her mate, leave her pack if need be, to be with him. But instead of fighting for her, he'd let a male he claimed to love like a brother take the fall. Though things had come crashing down in ways she'd never expected when her mate went to Thomas and admitted she was causing disloyalty amid the pack, and she thought she'd be happy as long as they could be together, Sara had lost all respect for him after that day. "I didn't feel much o' anything other than shock. Why? What does Lucian have tae do with anything?"

"I ken he's Finn's father."

"That's no' true. Jaime is Finn's father." And that was

the truth. Jaime had taken her back after everything that had happened, and he'd raised Finn as his own. Another prickle of unease swept up her spine again when Thomas just stared at her. "What?"

"Ye can be honest with me, Sara. It's been many years since all o' that unpleasant business. I'm no' going tae kick ye out o' the pack now, especially since yer mate took ye back into his home and his bed. Jaime is one o' my best wolves. If you go, so does he, 'n' I dinna want tae lose him." He voice deepened with emotion. "I ken why Brock did what he did. He is a worthy male. And tis nothing but a shame what happened between him and Lucian. I ken it all, Sara. Ye can be honest with me now."

It didn't hurt her feelings that he was worried about losing Jaime and not so much her. She and Thomas had always clashed. "All right. Fine. The truth o' it is, that was a verra confusing time for me. I dinna ken who is Finn's father by blood. I loved Lucian. And I dinna want Jaime tae find out. He would've killed him and ye ken it tae be true. The only way tae keep Jaime from suspecting anything was going on was tae continue tae be with him while I was with Lucian. I'm no' proud o' what I did. And if that makes me unworthy, than so be it. But I thought I was doing right by the male I loved at the time."

Looking away, she wiped at the tear that had escaped and was currently sliding down her cheek. This was ridiculous. All of that was in her past, and she was with the male she was supposed to be with. The fling with Lucian was just that…a fling. She had been young and naïve and entirely too full of herself.

He still was, from what she had seen.

"So, now that ye got what ye wanted out o' me, are ye going tae tell me why yer asking me about Lucian?"

"Do ye think he still has feelings for ye?"

"I wouldn't ken. And I dinna care one way or the other." She narrowed her eyes at him, suddenly suspicious. "Why do ye?"

Thomas sat back in his chair and regarded her with a steady stare. "I need ye tae bring Lucian back here."

"Me?" She laughed out loud. "Why dinna ye just ask him tae come for a visit?"

"That's no' how it works, and ye ken that."

She sobered at his serious tone. "What in the world makes ye think he would listen tae me? What happened between us was a long time ago, 'n' it did no' end well."

"If he has a soft spot for anyone here, it will be ye. And Finn."

Sara shoved her chair back and rose from the table. "No. Absolutely not. I am no' bringing my ten year old son in tae whatever ye got scheming around in yer head."

"I dinna remember asking."

The weight of the alpha's will forced her back into her chair. "Thomas, ye cannae be serious."

"Och. But I am. I need tae get Lucian here and back on our side, and ye and Finn are my best chance at doin' it." He took a deep breath and scrubbed his face with his hands.

Sara crossed her arms over her chest, refusing to look at him. How could he ask this of her? To use her son? "What about Jaime?"

"Jaime cannae ken."

Her head whipped back around. "Yer asking me tae betray the trust o' my mate…again…"

"If there was another way, Sara. I would do it. But there is no'. Ye ken Lucian. He is angry 'n' suspicious by nature. I'll never get him here any other way. Tell him about Finn. Invite him tae come home so he can get tae ken his son. Tis all I ask."

"And if that's no' enough?"

"Then you will do wha' ye have tae. But get him here."

CHAPTER 13

Keelin came out of the bathroom, if a toilet that was nothing more than a hole in the ground and a sink consisting of a bucket of water with a layer of ice on top to wash with could be called as much, and found an empty room waiting for her.

Lucian had been quiet and distant since the night before. After he'd apologized—for giving her the best sex of her life no less—he'd gotten up from the bed, found his jeans and boots and pulled on a shirt, and taken up a post by the door. She'd tried to talk to him a few times, had even gotten up and shivered her way across the room to him, only to be told to get back into the bed before she "froze her arse off".

He would keep watch.

Eventually, she'd rolled herself up in the sleeping bags like a burrito and dozed off. When she woke up to find him watching her, he'd let himself out the door without a word about where he was going or if or when he'd be back.

Now, in the frail light of early morning, she could see the storm had stopped, leaving a thick blanket of snow over the world. Keelin finished lacing up her boots and then stood in the center of the room, trying to decide if she should go look for him or just wait until he decided to come back.

Or, she could go back down the mountain, collect her things, drive into Darrington, and get a room at the Motor Inn until she could arrange to sell her house and start a new life far away from creatures like werewolves who shifted into sexy Scots and the rabid Fae he was determined to protect her from, but nothing more.

Option three was the most sane. Surely, those things that had come last night were long gone by now. Lucian wouldn't follow her. He'd be relieved she was out of his hair. And quite frankly, she was feeling a bit used and pretty pissed off right about now.

Fuck him. She didn't need a savior.

Taking a deep breath, she repeated those words over and over in her head until she halfway believed it to be true. She would go down the mountain. Once she hit the base, she would know where she was and could follow the tree line to her backyard. The heavy flannel shirt she'd found and now wore under her coat would help protect her from the cold, as would the exercise. Once she made it home, it wouldn't take her long to pack up some clothes and other personal items, grab her phone, get in her car, and go. She had snow tires. The roads would be plowed by the time she left. And there was a good amount of money in her savings account, enough that she could go anywhere she wanted and rent an apartment for a couple of months while she looked for a new job. And a new life.

At least for the time being.

She wondered if she should warn her neighbors. Not with the truth, of course. But she could tell them there was a rogue bear roaming around. A pack of rabid coyotes. Something. Anything. As long as it kept them inside.

Mind made up, she left the cabin without a backward glance at the bed where she had felt so much for the first time in over a year. Pausing on the porch just long enough to zip her coat and pull her hood up—twisting her long hair and tucking it inside—she shoved her hands in her pockets and stepped down into the snow. It wasn't as bad as she thought, only about eight or nine inches of accumulation. Hell, if she could find something flat and smooth, she could slide down the mountain.

"Where do ye think yer going?"

The words were little more than a growl directly behind her, but though her steps stuttered, she didn't stop or turn around. "I'm going home."

"Home, ye say?"

"Yes," she told him. "Home." She didn't bother to fill him in on the rest of her plan. She was no longer his concern, just how he wanted it. He'd made that abundantly clear.

Lucian was in front of her before she had a chance to hear him coming or see him move, looking way too yummy in a long-sleeved green shirt and jeans. She pulled up short just before her nose smashed into his chest.

Which was lucky, because he smelled *really* good. And that just made everything harder.

Keelin looked up at him, taking in the tightness around his eyes, the spots of color in his cheeks, and the hard line of his mouth. She narrowed her eyes at his expression. He wanted to be angry with her? Fine. He could be angry. But she was downright pissed off. "What." It wasn't exactly a question. More like a dare. But he answered her anyway.

"After everything I went through tae save yer hide last night, yer just going tae flounce on back down the mountain right in tae the waiting arms o' the soul suckers?"

"I'm not going to flounce," she informed him. "I'm going to slide." Stepping around him, she added, "And they're probably long gone by now."

"We dinna ken that."

"I *ken* I need to get the hell away from you."

"Keelin."

Pulling her hood down further in an attempt to block the wind, she ignored him and kept walking.

"Yer acting like a child," he shouted.

That stopped her. She spun around. "*I'm* acting like a child? Me? You're the one who's been giving me the silent treatment all night instead of communicating like a mature adult."

"Keelin…"

"Fuck off, Lucian." She was done with this conversation. Done with playing the helpless human. Keelin had no time for hot shifters with sad eyes who didn't know what they wanted.

Lucian appeared in front of her again.

This time, she threw her hands up and shoved him.

Her efforts were about as effective as they would be trying to push a brick wall out of the way, but she shoved him again anyway. "Stop doing that!"

He leaned down until they were nose to nose. "Then stop walking away 'n' listen tae what I'm trying tae say."

Keelin felt hot tears blurring her vision. She tried to blink them back before they fell, but it was too late. Lowering her chin, she wiped them away with the back of her hand, disgusted with herself and with him. She should not be this affected by some guy she barely knew. They'd had a total of...what...three, four, conversations? Including this one? Other than their combustible physical attraction, what did they have in common?

"Och, lass. Dinna cry. I cannae take yer tears."

Keelin sniffed and wiped at her eyes again, keeping her eyes down, she focused on their boots, standing toe to toe. "Nobody's asking you to. I just want to go home."

"Keelin..." He pressed his palms into either side of his head, then dropped his arms. "I'm sorry, lass."

"It's not your fault those things have it in for me."

"No' about that. Well, I am sorry about that, but that is no' what I'm sorry about."

She frowned up at him. "What does that even mean?"

He looked away, and his chest rose and fell with a great sigh. When his eyes came back to her, they were dark and stormy under his lowered brows, his mouth a tight line. "Ye do something tae me, Keelin. 'n' I dinna like it."

Despite her determination not to react, her heart swelled in her chest with his first statement, only to sink down to her stomach with the second. She lifted her chin.

"Is that supposed to be some kind of declaration of your feelings for me?"

"Aye. It is." He paused. Took a step back. Scrubbed his face with his hands. Pushed a wavy lock of red hair off his forehead.

Keelin watched his struggle, and wondered what caused it. Surely, all of this emotional turmoil wasn't because of her. Or at least, not only because of her. Not unless he knew she hadn't been exactly up front with him. But he couldn't know that. If he did, they wouldn't be standing there having this conversation.

"I'm sorry for the way I've been treating ye since… since…" His face turned as red as his hair. "Well, since last night. And I'm sorry for tha', tae." He threw his shoulders back and looked her in the eye then. "But I made a vow tae Cedric tha' I would keep ye safe, 'n' tha' is what I'm going tae do."

"You're…sorry? For sleeping with me?" Keelin couldn't remember a time when a man had ever apologized for giving her mind-blowing orgasms. Sloppy drunk sex when they really wanted to be with someone else? Sure. But not completely sober, bone-melting, beautiful, soul-crushing sex. "You're sorry."

"Aye, lass. I am. I'm no' normally tha'…weak."

Her own cheeks began to burn. Which was ridiculous. She was a grown female. There was no reason to be embarrassed about sex. "So, you don't normally…"

"No." He looked her right in the eye, his jaw tense and his cheeks flaming red. "I dinna."

"Oh. I see." And she did see. She saw exactly. Keelin lifted her chin, refusing to be ashamed for something beautiful and natural, or as natural as a Faerie and a shifter having sex could be. "Let's just chalk it up to exactly what it was, and move on. No apology is needed or necessary." She took a deep breath. "Thank you for helping me last night, but really, I'm okay on my own." With a last searching look at his shuttered expression, she turned away from him and started making her way down the mountain.

Her tears burned her eyes, and this time she let them fall. Keelin knew she was no great beauty men got stupid over. However, she wasn't young and naïve anymore, either. She was smart, and she was kind, and she loved with everything in her. If Lucian wanted to pass up on all of that, if his being attracted to her was nothing but a "weakness", then let him.

He didn't even try to stop her from leaving this time. And that told her everything she needed to know.

Her boot slid in the snow, and she reached out and grabbed the prickly trunk of an evergreen tree to stop her downward momentum. When she'd found her footing, she swiped at the moisture on her face with her free hand.

A huff of breath directly in front of her brought her head up fast, and she found herself face to face with a large, brown wolf. Its dancing green eyes glowed from within, much as Lucian's did when he was in his wolf form.

Keelin froze, staring at the creature that was so similar to him and yet, so different. She didn't know what to do. The wolf didn't appear threatening. It just stared at her with the same open curiosity she was giving it. Should she try to walk past? Turn her back on it and try to get back up the mountain to Lucian? Was he even still there?

Her question was answered when the wolf in question spoke from directly behind her.

"Och, Duncan. What the fook are ye doing here?"

The new wolf—Duncan?—shifted his eyes from her to Lucian, tongue hanging out of his open mouth like a dog. He lifted his nose, sniffing the air between them, and his jaw snapped shut. He chuffed low in his throat, then turned and began to pick his way silently through the snow-covered forest floor, heading west.

Lucian growled back. "It's no' yer fookin' business."

The other wolf gave him a glance and kept walking.

With an exasperated sigh, Lucian took her arm. "Come on, lass."

Keelin dug in her heels. "I'm not going that way. I'm going home."

"We dinna have time for this, Keelin."

"Then stop trying to force me to go with you. I'm not going with you. I'm going home."

"Lass, ye cannae stay in tha' house! The soul suckers may no' be there now, but they'll be back, I can guarantee it. They have ye on their radar now. I dinna ken how, or why, but they do. 'n' they dinna give up. They won't give up until they find ye." He took her hands in both of his own. "If ye stay here, they will find ye. If ye leave," he spoke over her as she began to protest. "They will follow ye, 'n' I will no' be there tae get ye out this time. Please, Keelin. Come with me now."

The sincerity in his eyes gave her pause. Was she being irrational? Risking her life over some hurt feelings? She glanced around his muscular arm at the wolf behind him, waiting impatiently.

Lucian followed her eyes, looking over his shoulder. He rolled his eyes when he saw what she was staring at. "Dinna worry about him. Tis only Duncan. He's one o' my pack. He will no' hurt ye."

"Why is he here?"

"Probably checking up on me when I did no' check in last night. I had my phone with me when I got ye out o' the house, but I lost it when I shifted. I did no' want tae leave ye alone tae go 'n' look for it."

Keelin felt a spot of warmth blossom in her chest at his words. Small, but there. She stared up into his stormy eyes. Eyes that so easily grew cold and distant, and she immediately chided herself. He didn't want to leave her because he'd promised his alpha he would make sure nothing happened to her. Not because of any sort of sappy feelings he had.

But, he was right about one thing. If what he said were true, and she had no reason to think he would be lying, it would be stupid for her to go back to her house, even to pack her things and leave.

"Okay."

"Okay?"

"Yeah. Fine. Let's go."

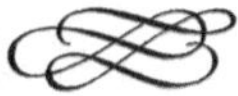

CHAPTER 14

Lucian kept hold of Keelin's hand the entire time they followed Duncan across the mountain. He told himself it was to make sure she didn't try to leave again, but it was a lie. He held it because he wanted to hold it. Wanted to have a physical connection with her, however small.

Duncan trotted through the snow ahead of them, looking for all the world like he was having the time of his life, instead of playing babysitter. Though his pack mate was a royal pain in the arse, for once, Lucian was happy he was there. If he wasn't, he would be tempted to do something about the fact that Keelin's hand was cold as ice—like stick it beneath his clothing where his overheated skin could warm it up. To be fair, he would do the same with the other hand. And perhaps her lips...they were looking a wee bit blue...

Hot desire boiled the blood in his veins at the memory of her running her tongue down his abs. Grinding his jaw together until his teeth ached, he pushed the fantasy from his mind. Keelin deserved better than a male who only rutted inside of her to find his own pleasure and leave her wanting. Shame doused the fire in his blood, but somehow it didn't quite get the message to his swollen cock.

Just ahead, a Jeep was parked dead center of the dirt road that wound up the mountain. The same dusky color of the evergreens surrounding it, it blended into the forest surrounding it. The thing had oversized tires, a hard top, and a roll bar, and it was Duncan's favorite toy.

And the owner of that toy was in the last stages of shifting right beside it.

Lucian heard Keelin's gasp of surprise, and stepped in front of her to block the other wolf from her view, but he hadn't counted on Duncan's bare arse strutting barefoot across the snow to open the back of the Jeep, lips pursed in a cheerful whistle. Just in case anyone might not have noticed him.

Lucian pushed Keelin further behind him, using his size to block the sight of the other male, unapologetically naked. Funny, he'd never really noticed the abundance of muscle the other male possessed, or how well-hung he was. "What the fook is wrong with ye, Duncan?"

Duncan stepped into a pair of loose, black running pants and pulled a T-shirt from the Jeep. He frowned over at Lucian. "Wha'?"

"Wha'?" Lucian mocked. "There's a wee lass here who's no' used tae our ways! 'n' yer prancing around with yer wanger swinging free!"

Duncan's head popped through the neckline of his

shirt, and a wide grin split his features. "Maybe the lass likes the sight o' my wanger."

A growl ripped through the air. "I dinna think so, ye arrogant bastard."

"How do ye ken?" Duncan pressed. "Did ye ask the lass in question?"

Only Keelin's tightened hold on his hand kept Lucian from springing across the thirty feet that separated them and taking Duncan's throat between his teeth.

"I didn't really see anything," she said from behind him. "But it's not like I haven't seen a naked man before. We're all adults here. There's no need to protect my sensibilities."

The humor in her voice brought heat to his cheeks. He was acting like he had some kind of right to her. To who or what she chose to look at…or more.

It was true, however, that Duncan didn't need to be any more full of himself than he already was. "Just put yer clothes on," Lucian growled.

Looking down at his covered form, Duncan threw his arms out to the sides and turned in a circle. "Are these no' clothes? Wha' am I missing?"

"Yer boots," Lucian told him. Moving out of the way, he led Keelin to the other side of the Jeep and put her in the backseat. It would've been more gentlemanly to let her sit in the front, but he couldn't stomach the thought of her any closer to Duncan—the bastard—than she absolutely had to be.

Besides, he was no gentleman.

"Where are you taking me?" she asked when he joined her in the Jeep.

"Tae our place, for now. If that's all right with ye? It's just outside the city, 'n' there are other females there." Later, he would tell her what sort of females. Once she'd met them and felt more comfortable.

Duncan got in the driver's side and started the Jeep. With a grin at Lucian, he swung it around and headed down the side of the mountain.

"How did ye find us?" Lucian asked.

"Wha'? Yer wee cabin? It's no' the first time I've been there, pup. I followed ye there the first time ye went running through these mountains."

Och. So, even the privacy he thought he had was nothing but an illusion.

"One question." Duncan took a hairpin turn going way too fast. "Why didn't ye just take the car, ye eejit? Instead o' dragging the poor lass up the mountain?"

Lucian rolled his eyes. "They'd follow her car, Duncan. Ye ken they would."

"Soul suckers are no' tha' smart."

"It wasn't only soul suckers coming after her. They had others leading them. I heard them ordering the sick ones about."

Duncan gave him a look of surprise. "No shite?"

"No shite." He wasn't a fucking idiot. If it had been safe to take the car, he would've taken the car.

They were down the mountain and heading west when Keelin spoke again. "So, how long have you guys been… uh…brothers? Litter mates?" She paused. "Sorry, I'm not sure what the correct wordage is here."

"Tae long."

"Long enough tae ken the lad has a good heart, if ye can get past the demons he battles."

Lucian looked over at Duncan in surprise. He'd always felt the other wolf had one purpose in life —to annoy him to the point of insanity. Never would he have thought Duncan had bothered to look any deeper. It made him uncomfortable, being analyzed like that. "Ye ken nothing about me, Duncan."

Duncan glanced over at him briefly before turning his eyes back to the road. "That's where ye would be wrong, pup."

From the corner of his eye, Lucian saw Keelin watching him. He didn't know what to say. And so he said nothing.

The rest of the ride passed in an awkward silence until they pulled up to their apartments.

"When you said you lived outside the city, I didn't realize you meant Seattle," Keelin said as Duncan parked the Jeep in the lot behind their small apartment building.

"Aye," Lucian told her. "It's close tae those Cedric thinks we need tae be close tae, 'n' still has plenty of wild land tae roam." Was she worried being so far from home? "But dinna fash yerself, lass. I can get ye back tae yer home in no time a'tall if something arises. 'n' I ken ye will need yer things. I can run for those as soon as ye get settled."

"You don't know where everything is. It would be easier if I came with you—"

He cut her off. "No, lass. It's tae dangerous. Ye'll be safer here with the others."

She looked as though she was about to argue, but luckily, Duncan interrupted whatever she'd been about to say.

Already out of the Jeep, Duncan peered through the window at them. "Are ye coming or wha'?"

"Aye!" Lucian got out of the Jeep, and after a moment, Keelin followed him. He had no wish to fight with her over this. But if need be, he would chain her to the bed in his apartment to keep her there. To keep her safe. And he would not feel a wee bit bad about it.

Once inside, they hit the stairwell. He didn't think about it. Lucian always preferred stairs over an elevator. Elevators were too easy to be trapped in. But he needn't have worried about it. Keelin kept up easily.

Cedric met them at the top. "Wha' happened, Lucian? Why is she here?"

He watched as Keelin's gaze traveled from Cedric's size sixteen boot, up his powerful body, to the top of his dark head. Her eyes widened when the pack leader's icy blues met hers. Perhaps bringing her here wasn't the very best of ideas. He should have kept her in that cabin. Or gotten a hotel. But he didn't have his phone or his wallet, and he couldn't very well allow the lass to freeze and starve. "They were comin' for her. I had tae get her out o' her place fast."

"Why didn't ye call?"

"I lost my phone."

"He lost his phone when he shifted to fight off one of those things. It followed us from my house."

Cedric turned those eerie eyes to Keelin. "Forgive me, lass." He stuck out his hand. "I'm Cedric. I'm the' pack master—"

Keelin took his hand as though she were uncertain whether she should or not. "I know who you are, Cedric

Kincaid. My mother spoke highly of you. She said you were not just painfully attractive and strong, but a good and fair pack leader." Her cheeks flushed, and Lucian barely caught his growl of displeasure before it burst from his throat. A blatant threat to his alpha. "It appears she was right. At least on the first two counts."

He lifted one eyebrow. "Did she, now? Yer maw was a braw woman." He shifted on his feet slightly. "It sounds like tae me."

Lucian stepped slightly in front of Keelin, laying his claim without properly thinking about it. "I thought I would keep Keelin here. Just for now. I hadn't planned on it, but I dinna ken where else tae take her."

Cedric leveled him with a steady stare. "This is no' the best place for yer lass."

"She's no' *my* lass." A noise from Keelin had him turning to look at her, but she quickly dropped her eyes, hiding herself from him. He turned back to his alpha. "Those things ken where she lives, Cedric. I dinna ken where they came from, or why, or how, but they're here. Someone is directing them, 'n' for reasons unbeknownst tae us, they're after Keelin herself."

From his side, Keelin spoke up. "It's okay. I don't need to stay here. If someone could just go back to my house and get my things and my car, I can leave."

"Cedric, ye ken they will find her wherever she goes. It's no' safe for her out there. This is the safest place for her."

Looking back and forth between them, Cedric suddenly leaned down until his nose was between his arm and Keelin's shoulder. He took a deep breath, and his big body became completely still. Slowly, his head turned until he pegged Lucian with disbelieving eyes. "It can no' be." He straightened to his full, impressive height, and Lucian felt the will of the alpha pressing on him. "Lucian, ye can no' get involved with this female."

"Wha' I did or dinna do with her is o' no concern. It does no' change anything."

Keelin frowned. "How do you all know something happened?"

Cedric gave her a sad smile and tapped the side of his nose.

"Oh."

Her blush reddened her cheeks and neck, and Lucian wanted very badly to see what other parts of her were colored with it. He tore his eyes away from the intriguing sight, and tried to get the conversation back to what was important.

"Cedric. I can no' just let her go off on her own. Ye are the one who insisted I keep an eye on her. If Keelin is so verra important tae ye, this is the safest place for her tae stay until we can work something else out." He held his breath as Cedric glanced back and forth between the two of them, obviously weighing his options.

Duncan spoke up. "The lad is right, Cedric. She will be safe here until we chase the fuckers off."

Cedric never took his eyes from Keelin. "Safe from the soul suckers, aye. It's no' them I'm worried about."

Lucian felt his hackles go up. "If it's me yer blathering about, I dinna see why ye gave me the job in the first place if ye dinna trust me tae keep her safe."

The weight of the alpha lifted until only the slightest

emphasis remained. "No, Lucian. It's no' ye I'm speaking o'." A smile crinkled the skin at the corners of his eyes. "Tae be true, yer the safest one for her tae be with. I trust ye completely with her well-being." Hands on his hips, he nodded thoughtfully. "Aye. Take her tae yer place."

"I'm standing right here, you know," Keelin told them both. "And I'm capable of making my own decisions. I'm actually quite intelligent."

Cedric turned to her. "My apologies, lass. Keelin," he emphasized. "If ye agree, I think it would be safest for ye tae stay with Lucian. At least, for now. Duncan can go get yer things from yer house 'n' even bring yer car here for ye, if tha' will make ye feel more comfortable. We're only looking out for ye. Truly."

Keelin and Cedric stared at each other, and Lucian got the feeling something was passing between them. Some kind of communication he was completely missing.

"Okay," she told him after a pause.

Cedric gave her a nod. "Duncan, would ye join me, please?" With a slap on Lucian's shoulder, he said his goodbyes.

The decision was made. And even though it had been Lucian's idea to bring her here, he felt the familiar needles of frustration prick his nerves. What he didn't know, was why.

Left alone with Keelin, he realized he was standing there fuming while she stood waiting. With a mumbled apology, he directed her down the hall to his apartment, praying to all the gods they didn't run into anyone else on the way. There were things that needed to be said, and he needed to stop being such a pussy and say them.

But when he got her inside and had her alone, he found he wasn't so brave after all.

"So, they can smell you on me, huh?" Keelin walked away before he could answer, exploring his small kitchen. It was clean and modern. And cold, he suddenly realized, with its white cabinets and gray countertops. Not in temperature, but in feeling.

He glanced toward the living room just beyond. It was no better. Though the entire place was clean enough to eat off the floors, thanks to Bronaugh's Aunt Nancy, it was furnished with only the bare necessities, the couch the same gray as the counters and the floor. No television. No reading nook.

Truth be told, Lucian didn't spend a lot of time here. He much preferred running free in the misty mountains rising majestically outside the window.

"I don't mind." Keelin turned and leaned back against the sink, reminding him of the kiss they'd shared in a different kitchen. A much warmer kitchen. Unlike that night, the look in her eye now was downright sinful. "That I smell like you."

"Keelin." Her name was wrung from his throat, brought on by too many emotions. Lucian liked her smelling like him, too.

She came toward him, walking slow…hesitating… killing him with the waiting.

But when she finally reached him, he shook his head. Took a step back. Not because he didn't want her close to him, but because he wanted to express to her how badly he felt about the way he'd acted the night before. Wanting to make it up to her. "I'm sorry, lass."

"I can feel you tremble when I touch you, you know." To prove this fact, she laid her palms flat on his chest. They rose up and down with his quick breaths. "If you're about to tell me you don't 'feel that way' about me, you're lying."

Och. He wished he could tell her that. He truly did. Because what was happening inside of him would only complicate things more than they needed to be. What if Cedric decided she was a threat to them? What if she decided being with him was too outside of her realm of reality?

What if he got too attached.

But…ah, *gods*. He did so love it when she touched him.

"Last night—"

He didn't let her finish, needing to say what he wanted to say before he lost himself in her. "I am truly sorry about tha'." He moved her long hair from her shoulder, exposing the pulse in her throat to his hungry gaze. "I dinna ken what came over me."

Keelin stared up at him, and her eyes were the turquoise blue of the sea rolling with waves of darker green. He inhaled her sweet honey flower scent. It wasn't something artificial, like a lotion or perfume. It was her own natural fragrance. Gods, it made his mouth water.

"If you apologize to me one more time for the *fucking magical* sex we had last night, Lucian Kincaid, I'm going to punch you right in the mouth."

Her words caught him unawares, but he quickly recovered. "Ye dinna mean that, lass. Ye'll break the wee bones in yer hand."

"Oh, but I do."

CHAPTER 15

A smile tugged at the corners of his mouth. "Twas magical, ye say?"

Though she tried to hang on to the frustration, Keelin felt it drain away with one look at the light fighting its way through the storm in his eyes. "Yes," she told him in all seriousness. "It was. And I really wish you'd stop apologizing for making love to me."

A frown extinguished the light she loved. "Ye misunderstand, lass. I'm no' telling ye I wish it didn't happen. I just should've done better by ye, is all. I ken I left ye unsatisfied, and tha's what I'm apologizing for. It's been a while for me, 'n' ye are…"

Heat rose to the surface of her skin as his eyes left trails of fire from the top of her head to her thighs.

"Yer all woman, lass. Yer my dirtiest fantasies come true." He paused. Looked away. Cleared his throat. "I'm sorry, I'm no' good with words. But, I dinna ken how else tae say it."

Keelin covered his mouth with her hand. "You're saying it just fine." Tears pricked the back of her eyes. The raw emotion with which he spoke said it so much better than all the flowery words she read in her romance novels. Told her so much more. All of her insecurities faded away beneath the burning need in his expression.

She opened her mouth. Words of her own bubbled to the surface, words that would tell him who and what she truly was, only to catch in her throat when he beat her to it.

"I'd be honored if ye would allow me tae kiss ye right now."

He honestly appeared terrified she would refuse him. And she knew without a doubt that if she did, he would back down without complaint. Keelin stepped into him until her breasts brushed his shirt. She ran her hands up his arms, feeling the muscles tremble beneath her palms. Leaning in, she pressed her lips to the warm skin at the base of his throat.

Gooseflesh rose on his skin beneath her fingers as Lucian sucked in a breath and held it. His large body went perfectly still, waiting to see what she would do next.

Confidence rose, knowing how she affected him by something so simple as a touch. Emboldened by his reaction, Keelin dropped her hands to the bottom of his shirt. As she felt for the edge, the back of her fingers brushed the hard ridge straining against the front of his jeans and he moaned, but still didn't move. Sliding her hands beneath his shirt, Keelin found the warm skin of his hard abs. Tentatively, she explored the ridges of muscle with her fingertips, following them around to the sides and up to his pecs and hard shoulders.

When she finally got up the nerve to glance at his face, she found she needn't have worried. His eyes were closed, his mouth slightly open as he fought for breath. Keelin let her hands slide back down his chest and stomach, watching his reaction. When she reached the waistline of his jeans, she paused briefly. Leaving one hand on his hip, she brushed her palm over him.

A low growl purred deep in his throat, and he opened his eyes.

Though his arms still hung at his sides and not so much as a muscle moved other than his eyes, Keelin felt a small tinge of panic when she found herself staring into the hungry gaze of the wolf.

Is this what had made love to her the night before? It had been so dark she hadn't been able to see very much, only feel. And what she'd felt was a frantic need, a flood of emotions, and an unnatural strength that he'd tried his best to contain, though he hadn't quite succeeded. If Keelin were truly only human, it's very likely she wouldn't have come out of that experience as unscathed as she had.

His upper lip lifted into a snarl, and his eyes dropped to her breasts. He moved then, lifting his hand to touch her.

A hard knock at the door had Keelin stepping back from him so fast she slammed her backside into the handle of the oven. Lucian stayed right where he was, his eyes glowing with an unholy light as they traveled down the length of her and back.

The knock came again.

With a low growl of displeasure, he spun on his heel and stalked over to the door, leaving Keelin feeling as though she'd just barely missed being swept away by a category five hurricane.

Bending at the waist, she braced her hands on her knees and took a few deep breaths. Sweet hell, one riled up look from that male and her heart was racing like she'd just survived the zombie apocalypse. Voices came from the entryway, his and a female's. By the time he returned, Keelin was casually leaning against the counter, her arms crossed over her stomach to hide the tremors.

"Keelin, this is Bronaugh."

A Fae female with medium length, wheat-blonde hair and brown eyes came around him, hand stuck out for Keelin to shake. The female was just slightly shorter than her, with full hips and thighs, and when Keelin unwrapped one arm and took her hand, she caught a whiff of meadowsweet flowers. A shockwave shot through her, but Keelin only smiled. "Hello, Bronaugh. It's nice to meet you. I'm Keelin Doran."

A kaleidoscope of colors flashed briefly in the other female's eyes before she could control it, leaving no doubt as to what type of Faerie she was. She squinted at Keelin, but followed her lead. "Hi, Keelin." Bronaugh took her hand and squeezed it. "Bronaugh Lane." Then she smiled and turned back to Lucian. "Cedric asked me to come and keep her company while you and Duncan go check out her place and get her car and shit."

Lucian's eyes went to Keelin, and he didn't even try to hide the hunger lighting them from within.

Bronaugh looked back and forth between them. "Duncan's waiting for you," she told him in a bored tone.

"Och, aye," he ground out. "I'll be right back." This was directed at Keelin. With a distrustful glance at Bronaugh that spoke volumes about his feelings toward her, he left.

After he'd gone, Bronaugh walked over and locked the door, then came back to Keelin. Grabbing an apple from the bowl on the counter, she mimicked Keelin's relaxed pose. "So! Why is everyone lying to Lucian?" She took a bite of the apple. Juice ran down her chin. "Including you." Wiping it away with the back of her hand, she took another bite. "When it's blatantly obvious you want that strapping wolf bod."

Keelin thought about how she should answer that. If that little eye trick was any indication, this female was not only a Faerie, but a Dark Faerie. However, Keelin could've said what Bronaugh was the moment she touched her hand. She could feel the darkness churning around inside of her. It spoke to her own murky blood. Nature's way of alerting her when another of her kind was near. "Why haven't you told them how you're struggling with your sinister side?"

Bronaugh cocked her head and eyed her. "How do you know I haven't?"

"Because if you had, you wouldn't be standing here right now."

The other female chewed on her apple, her eyes never leaving Keelin. When she was done eating, she swallowed, tossed the core in the garbage under the sink, and turned her back to wash her hands. Drying them on the towel left beside the sink, she refolded it and leaned against the sink with her hands in the back pockets of her jeans. "Let's not fight," she told Keelin. "I think I like you."

"I think I like you, too," Keelin told her with a grin. "But, seriously, what's with all the subterfuge?"

"I'll tell you mine if you tell me yours."

"Deal."

Bronaugh came toward her, spit into the center of her palm, and held her hand out to shake again.

Keelin looked down at that hand in disgust. "Ew…really?"

"Shake, or no deal."

"I can't believe I'm doing this." Trying not to think about it, Keelin spit and clasped hands with the female.

"That was really gross," Bronaugh laughed, and washed her hands again.

Keelin joined her at the sink. "So, now you have to tell me. What's going on with you? And how did a Faerie girl end up here with a bunch of werewolves?"

"Probably the same way you're here. I fell in love with one of them."

Keelin laughed as she dried her hands. "Oh, I'm not in love with Lucian. And that's not why I'm here."

Bronaugh rolled her eyes. "Whatever."

"I'm not." She frowned when Bronaugh gave her a look that told her she didn't believe her at all. "And we're not talking about me right now. We're talking about you."

With a drawn out sigh, Bronaugh stared down at the floor.

Keelin felt a twinge of pity for her. "You need to tell them. Or tell your mate."

"Marc."

"Marc. Tell Marc. If he loves you, he'll help you."

Bronaugh laughed without humor. "How is he supposed to help me? He can't stop what I am. What I'm becoming," she corrected.

"Maybe not, but he needs to know. You're putting them all in danger."

Bronaugh looked straight at her then. "No more than you are, my new friend."

"I'm not like you."

"No, you're not. But I know what you are. Or should I say, *who* you are."

Keelin started to shake her head. There was no way this Faerie she'd just met had any idea who she was. She'd been hidden her entire life.

"You're The Key."

Okaaay…maybe she did know. But she wasn't giving anything away until she knew for sure. "I'm not—"

"Pfft. Don't try to bullshit me, Keelin. Your mother was the one who locked up my people the first time. And when they break free, you'll be expected to do it again." She paused. "Maybe I'll be one of them this time."

Okay. Maybe she did know. Chewing her lip, Keelin eyed the pretty blonde. "Does this mean we can't be friends?"

"I don't see why it should. I mean, I'm mated to a werewolf and am the adopted niece of two very nice Fae of the *na maithe*. Why the hell shouldn't I be friends with you?" She grinned.

Keelin grinned back. She really did like this female.

"Your turn. What are you doing here and why is everyone lying to Lucian?"

She told Bronaugh about Lucian coming to her rescue, how he'd fought off the first two soul suckers, then saved her again and hidden her in the cabin, standing guard all night until Duncan came for them the following day. "He told me Cedric ordered him to protect me, but didn't seem to know why." She gave a little shrug as she said, "Knowing Lucian's reputed hatred of our kind, I thought it better not to tell him who, or what, I am." A glimmer of hope sparked within her. "But, maybe now, seeing as to how you live here and everything, he wouldn't take it so badly?"

"Oh, hell no. He still hates us." Bronaugh yawned, obviously unconcerned. "He would kill me in a heartbeat if he thought he could get away with it. But he is pretty fond of my Aunt Nancy, the female who adopted me. She puts him in his place." She grinned. "I miss her. She and my uncle moved down south to be closer to their daughter."

But Keelin wasn't ready to give up just yet. "But, how can he not tell what I am? He's a shifter. A werewolf. His kind are raised to hunt my kind."

"I think your smell confuses him. If you were only *an olc* or only *na maithe*, he would know for sure."

Keelin didn't buy it. Yet, he'd treated her as human this entire time. He wasn't faking it.

"Or," Bronaugh continued. "Maybe he's in denial. He doesn't want you to be a creature he hates. Because if you were, he wouldn't be able to love you."

"Ha! Lucian does *not* love me."

"He lusts after you."

Keelin couldn't deny that fact.

"The love will come. Although if he's like a certain

other werewolf I know, it might take him a minute to realize what it is."

"And what do I do until then?"

"Pray to the gods he doesn't find out what you are before then."

CHAPTER 16

Lucian took the lead as he and Duncan came up on Keelin's property. They'd run the entire way, stopping only once at the cabin to shift back and dress, and it still wasn't enough to douse the fire in Lucian's blood caused by Keelin's gentle exploration back in his apartment.

His cock, like the rest of him, was a wee bit hard to discourage.

They'd taken the same route Lucian had the first time he'd seen her, and now, as they reached the base of the mountain where it opened up to the mowed field that served as her back yard, Duncan stopped him with a hand on his shoulder.

The late afternoon sun was in Lucian's eyes, so at first he didn't know why they were stopping.

And then the wind shifted.

"Is tha'—"

"Duana."

"Why is she here? At Keelin's home?" He'd very nearly said "my Keelin", but had stopped himself just in time to avoid the knowing looks Duncan was sure to shoot his way with that slip up.

"I dinna ken. But let's no' let her ken we are here just yet."

"Aye," Lucian agreed.

They crept forward as far as they could while staying in the cover of the large ferns that covered the ground. With the sun shining, the trees created plenty of shadows to hide them.

The stench of meat left too long in the sun hit his nose, and Lucian pulled Duncan down lower into the foliage.

But he needn't have worried, for the three soul suckers that stumbled out the back door behind the princess were well under control. It wasn't chains that held them, however. It appeared to be nothing more than the will of the lovely female they stood before, shifting restlessly from foot to foot as they waited for...what? Instruction? To be released?

Lucian stared in disgust at the scene playing out before him. As he watched the princess and her pets, he realized these soul suckers were not as mindless as most. Actually, now that he thought about it, the ones who had come after Keelin most definitely had a glimmer of sanity in their bloodshot, yellowed eyes. The first night and the last.

What in all the hell was going on? And out of all the humans on this green earth, why were they after her?

"It appears the princess is no' as loyal as she claims," Duncan stated the obvious.

"Did ye ever truly think she was?" Lucian made a

sound of disbelief and shook his head. It never ceased to boggle his mind how a male as intelligent as Cedric could be swayed by a sweet, lying mouth and a few womanly curves. "Tha' female does no' care about us, or the prince, or anything except her own. Though ye have tae admit, she has some balls, comin' out here in the middle o' the day."

"Aye. Tha' she does." He fell quiet for a moment, but then whispered, "I guess I cannae blame her for sticking by her own. I would probably do the same if in her position."

Lucian cast him a look, but didn't get a chance to reply, for right at that moment the princess turned her head and stared directly at the place they were hiding.

He held his breath, as did Duncan beside him, certain she had heard them. It wasn't that he was afraid of the wee female. Not even with all of her Dark magic. He just didn't want to have to tell Cedric they'd had to kill her. But the alpha's one weakness was very plain to see here—he always tried to see the good in others, even when there was none there to be found.

The Dark Fae princess held up her hand, ordering the others to be silent while she searched the trees. Turning her face away just slightly, she whispered something to the soul suckers. They immediately jumped down from the porch and headed straight toward the trees.

Lucian began to back away, as did Duncan, keeping their heads down and their movements silent. There was no way to know for sure if she had seen them or was just acting on instinct, but either way, it was time for them to leave. As it was, the gig would soon be up. The

Faeries would smell them as soon as they got a few yards closer.

A noise to their left froze Lucian where he was. He heard Duncan's swift indrawn breath just before he saw her. A lass with skin like snow and a head of dark curls pulled back on the crown of her head. She was crouched on the ground, staring at them with wide, dark eyes. Wearing a long-sleeved shirt and pants that hugged her skin, her clothing had a camouflage pattern that blended with the forest around them. She straightened, looked out at the soul suckers coming ever closer, and took off through the trees with such speed it left Lucian questioning whether he'd actually seen her or not.

He hit Duncan on the arm, and had to do it again when the wolf stayed as he was, staring into the trees in the direction the girl had gone. With a low growl, he finally got his attention and tugged him off in the opposite direction.

Running silently, dodging tree trunks and clumps of blackberry briars, they skirted the base of the mountain until they found a stream. The water was freezing cold, but Lucian plunged in without pause and sloshed upstream with Duncan right behind him. On the other side, they stripped, piling up their clothes on the ground. Gritting his jaw against the pain, he shifted into his preferred form and waited for Duncan to do the same. Lucian picked up his clothes and boots in his mouth and kept going. Duncan fell into step a little ways behind him. The older, stronger wolf protecting the younger. It was the way of the wolves.

He didn't stop until he reached the greenbelt behind

their apartments. By the time Duncan joined him again, he had dropped his clothes and was waiting. With a nod of his large head, Duncan let him know it was okay. They hadn't been followed this far.

His body was exhausted and his head was spinning, so it took him a minute to be able to shift again. And once he could manage it, the change was long and painful. Picking up his clothes, only slightly damp in a few spots, he got dressed and slid his feet into his boots.

"We need tae tell Cedric." Duncan buttoned the blue flannel shirt he'd borrowed back at the cabin.

"Aye. No' that he will listen."

"Oh, he'll listen. He just may no' do anything about it."

Lucian couldn't keep the look of disgust from his face. "O' course no'."

Duncan gave him a look he couldn't quite interpret. "Dinna judge so soon, pup. Let's see wha' he says." He cracked his neck and rolled his shoulders. "Come on."

As Lucian came up alongside him, Duncan glanced at him sideways. "Who do ye suppose tha' female was? The one who fell from the sky."

"I think it was a tree she fell from."

"It does no' matter where she fell from. Who do ye think she was?"

Lucian shrugged. Some lost female wasn't his concern right now. "I dinna ken, though she had the look o' the Fae about her."

Duncan nodded, his expression thoughtful. "Aye. She did at tha'."

His mind on Keelin, Lucian said offhandedly, "Maybe she was there with Duana."

But Duncan shook his head. "She was running from them, same as us." He paused. "Why would she be running? 'n' why didn't she let on she was there? Say something?"

"I dinna ken, Duncan. It's no' important."

Duncan raised an eyebrow at his tone. "It might be important."

"It's no'."

They reached the back door that led inside of their building. As Lucian put in the code and held it open, Duncan said, "Let's no' tell Cedric about her. I'll find out more about her first."

Lucian sighed heavily. "Fine. We will no' tell Cedric about her."

Once inside, he went straight to his apartment, ignoring Duncan's protests, and checked on Keelin. He found her curled up on the couch with Bronaugh, drinking tea and chatting about some show about a bachelor trying to date twenty different women. When Keelin saw him, she jumped up and set her cup down on the end table. "Lucian! What's wrong? Are you okay?"

He hadn't said a word, and yet she knew something had happened. "I'm sorry, lass. I dinna get any o' yer things. Or yer car. There was…something going on at yer house. I need tae go see Cedric 'n' let him know. I'll go back for ye."

"She can borrow some of my clothes," Bronaugh said. "Or better yet," She turned a bright smile to Keelin. "We can go shopping in Seattle!"

Lucian was struck with nerves at the thought. "She's no' going anywhere like tha'," he said. "It's no' safe."

Bronaugh rolled her eyes, but admitted, "You're probably right. If I know my people, and I do, they'll find her soon enough without putting her out there for all to see." She grabbed Keelin's hand to get her attention. "You can borrow some of my stuff. You don't even have to leave the building. Marc and I live right here."

Keelin smiled down at her. "Thank you."

Lucian frowned at something Bronaugh had said, but he couldn't quite put his finger on it. But whatever it was, he didn't like it. "Ye can go now, Bronaugh."

She raised an eyebrow at him, but got up, nonetheless. "Come over when you can, Keels, and we'll pick out some clothes."

Keelin smiled at her. "I will. Thanks."

He wanted to tell her she didn't need to borrow clothes, he would get her her own. But he didn't know when that would be. And he couldn't have her running around bare-arsed.

Mostly because he didn't want anyone else to see her that way, he was male enough to admit.

He needed to get to Cedric's. The alpha would have questions, and wouldn't appreciate him stopping here first. But he'd needed to reassure himself that the lass was okay, and that Bronaugh hadn't been up to any funny business. He trusted that Fae about as much as he trusted it not to rain in Pacific Northwest in the winter.

"So, what happened at my prouse?"

She looked okay after her visit with the Fae, only concerned for her home and things. And perhaps for him? "There were Faeries there."

"The things that came after me?"

"Like them, aye, but no' the same ones." He couldn't say anymore. Not yet. Wanting to greet her properly, but still not feeling comfortable doing so despite all that had happened between them, Lucian remained where he was. However, he could not keep himself from studying every inch of her, searching for clues that some harm had come to her while he'd been gone. When he found no sign of anything, he breathed a sigh of relief.

"Lucian—"

"I have tae go see Cedric 'n' let him know what happened." He felt like he was repeating himself. Had he said that already? "I'll be back as soon as I can."

Keelin took a seat on the sofa again, her eyes never leaving him. "Okay. I'll wait here."

He gave her a nod and left.

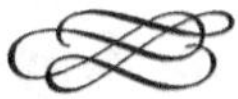

CHAPTER 17

We're all going to fookin' die because these eejits are tae blind tae see beyond the needs of their cocks.

Lucian rolled his head on his shoulders as a shudder overtook him. Skin slid over muscle that at once expanded and contracted before settling into its natural form again. He'd never get used to the feeling, no matter how many years he lived or how often it happened. But the peace that came with sloughing off his humanity was completely worth the pain of shifting. Forcing himself to calm, he fought the change that was as natural to him as breathing until he could get out of sight and not have to deal with the talking to he'd be sure to get from Cedric for not controlling his wolf.

While the rest of his pack hung out in the clearing, chatting it up like old friends with neighboring alphas and Fae alike, he made his way steadily into the cover of the trees. It wasn't natural, what they were doing. Packs existed for *a reason*. Wolves stuck to their own kind for *a reason.* Cedric, his alpha, was too open minded, too easily swayed. First befriending the bloodsuckers and now the Fae. Nothing good would come of it all. And by the time they all realized it, it would be too late.

After he and Duncan told him what they'd seen at Keelin's house, his solution was to call a meeting with the Fae and just...*ask*...Duana why she was there. When confronted, the lies flew from her mouth with ease, telling them she had only gone there because she knew Lucian had been hanging around there on his orders, and she'd wanted to find out why he'd taken such an interest in a human.

When asked about the soul suckers who'd been with her, she'd admitted they were there, and made her case on how she could "help" those who were succumbing to the sickness. Just like she had with those two. And promised both Cedric and Prince Nada that they could meet them soon.

Cedric was drowning under the spell of that Fae lass. Listening to the blood pounding through his cock rather than considering the needs of those who depended on him to lead. He saw the way the alpha couldn't take his eyes from the princess. And she was *an olc*! One of the Dark Fae! Lucian didn't care what kind of tale they tried to weave about how she'd been rescued during the first war and had come to see the error of her ways. He didn't care that she'd come to the gathering with Prince Nada, the Fae prince of the *na maithe* tribe. He didn't trust her. He didn't trust any of them. They didn't have to have the sickness to be dangerous. To be honest, he preferred the soul suckers. At least, once a Dark Fae had succumbed to the addiction, you knew what those ones were after.

They didn't smile to your face and slaughter your family behind your back.

Despite the sunny day, there was no moon tonight, but he didn't need the light it would provide, he could make out the shapes of the towering pines just fine. And he would be able to see even better as soon as he could give in to the rage burning through his veins. The others wouldn't notice his absence. They were too busy pretending an alliance between the packs was possible. That an alliance with the *Fae* was possible. That fucking their females and listening to their lies wasn't wrong.

But Lucian knew better. He'd seen with his own eyes what those bloody bastards were capable of.

A growl of frustration tore through his chest before he could stop it. They were all so fucking stupid. Magic had them all fooled. And Brock, his oldest friend, he was the worst of them all! For he'd fookin' started this whole mess when he'd followed his own Faerie lass right into another dimension. He was lucky to have lived through it with his limbs and mind still intact. If he had just let her be and hadn't followed Heather straight to Prince Nada in the first place, they wouldn't be mixed up in this shite.

Lucian didn't understand it. Not at all. Brock, out of all of them, should know better. He had been there, hiding with Lucian when the fuckers destroyed their home. Killed their pack.

A branch snapped behind him and Lucian spun around, dropping down into a crouch, ready to launch himself at the threat.

Duncan held both hands up in front of him, his face split into its usual wide grin, green eyes dancing with humor. "Whoa, easy there, lad. Ye dinna wanna do that, now. Ye ken I'll kick yer arse."

Lucian straightened. He didn't have time for this. "Leave me alone, Duncan." He spun on his heel and continued on his way, shoving sodden branches and brush out of his way, delving deeper into the thick pines covering the mountain, hoping for once Duncan would have the common decency to do as he'd asked.

But he should've known it wouldn't be that easy. Duncan caught up to him easily. "Where is it yer off to in such a hurry? 'n' why do ye look like yer ready to skin the hide off 'o' some poor, unsuspecting soul?"

"Away wit' ye, Duncan. I dinna need ye constantly up me arse!"

"Och. I think ye do. Lord knows what kind o' trouble ye'd get into if I wasn't here. Just look wha' happened when ye went tae save Keelin."

Lucian's head was on the verge of exploding. Spinning around so fast even Duncan lifted an eyebrow in surprise, he got right up in the other wolf's face. "I dinna need ye tae babysit me," he ground out. "Now, away wit' ye, afore ye cause me tae lose my temper."

Duncan grinned. "It's a wee bit too late for that, by the looks o' it."

If he lays one fookin' paw on me, I swear tae all the gods...

But with his typical intuition, Duncan seemed to know when he'd pushed Lucian to his limits, for he took a step back. A small concession. "Look," he said. "I ken why yer angry. But runnin' off half-cocked is no' going tae solve anything. And Cedric was asking where ye'd run off tae."

"Well, when he's done making an arse out o' himself over tha' *an olc* bitch, he can come 'n' find me."

"I dinna think that's a very nice thing tae say, Lucian. We dinna ken why she was there at Keelin's house." He shrugged. "Maybe she was telling the truth."

"She's *an olc*, a dark one. Tis all I need tae ken tae prove she's a liar. 'N' Cedric is a fool if he thinks she is anything worth gettin' tae know."

"Ye have an opinion about who I choose tae speak tae, pup?"

The smile fell from Duncan's face as the timbre of their alpha's voice rattled Lucian's bones. A crushing weight settled over him, and he fought the need to take on a submissive posture until his body shook with the effort and he could resist no longer.

Head bowed, he snarled, "Nothin' ye dinna already ken, Cedric."

Footsteps approached, though he would never have heard them if he didn't have the superior hearing of his kind. It always amazed him, how quietly the pack leader could move over twigs and leaves and rocks littering the ground beneath the trees, despite his size, when something as wee as a squirrel sounded like a heard of elephants crashing through the underbrush.

When Cedric spoke again, the deep growl was easier to understand, but the oppression of his will remained. "Och, aye. I ken ye dinna like the Fae folk. And I ken ye have yer reasons. They're good, solid reasons, Lucian. But these particular faeries are no' the ones who did that tae ye. They are no' the ones who took yer first pack from ye. Brock kens that. So does the rest o' the pack. Ye need tae get the same through yer thick skull. I'm growing tired o' defending myself 'n' my actions tae ye." He stepped closer, until Lucian had to crank his head back to see his face or stare at the veins bulging from his alpha's neck.

But Lucian refused to step back. "Perhaps ye feel the need tae defend yerself because ye ken ye should no' be gallivanting around with these creatures." He met the icy eyes of his pack leader. "Ye cannae trust them, Cedric! No matter what yer cock might be tellin' ye."

Cedric leaned down into his face, close enough Lucian could smell the whiskey on his breath from the shot he'd taken with Prince Nada, pulled out of thin air with the dark magic of the Fae. "I am no' ignorant, Lucian. I ken what the Fae are capable o'. Ye need tae trust me. Or ye need tae go find yerself another pack. One back in yer homeland, far away from this upcoming war. This rebellious attitude o' yours is going tae get us all killed!"

Killed? He was trying to protect them! Didn't Cedric see that? "I would no' *ever* endanger the pack, Cedric."

"Ye wouldn't mean tae, I ken that. But if ye cannae learn tae trust me, 'n' *obey*, without running off half-cocked 'n' questioning every decision I make, it *will* happen. Eventually." Cedric finally stepped back, and Lucian pulled much-needed air into his lungs as the will of the alpha eased off. "If tha' happens, Lucian, ye will have no one tae blame but yerself. Ye willnae be able tae put all yer hatred on the Fae like ye do now. No matter if they did anything personally tae ye or no'. Do ye ken?"

That wasn't going to happen. Any hatred he aimed at those fucking Fae would be well deserved.

"Lucian!"

"Aye!" he barked. "I ken." And he did. Better than any of them knew.

Cedric looked as though he wanted to say more. He glanced over at Duncan, who remained just out of the way should a fight break out, eyes on the ground. With a sigh, he turned back to Lucian. "Och, aye. Go on with ye, then. Have a good run. Get it out o' yer system. Then get yer arse back tae my place. We need tae speak about Keelin."

Without another word, Lucian broke into a jog and left them standing there. But he felt their condemning stares, and got as far as he could before he allowed the change to happen. With a moan that was a mixture of rage and relief, he gave in to the agonizing hedonism of shifting.

When it was done, he shook off the lingering tremors sliding up and down his spine, then threw his head back and howled the remaining vestiges of his human emotions to the night sky.

Coyote scattered throughout the mountains answered his call. Bears chuffed from a cluster of briars nearby as they scoured for the last remaining food before settling down to hibernate for the winter. Owls ghosted silently through the tall pines to observe this newcomer, and a fox yipped in warning as it ran away. Lucian's ears picked up the crunch of leaves as a deer ran through the underbrush a mile away, and his breath misted on the chill damp air as he growled deep in his throat, a hunter sensing his prey. Winter was well upon them, along with the rains that came here in the Pacific Northwest, and as it grew colder, many creatures of the forest would keep to their homes until the warmth of spring returned.

But not tonight. Tonight he would run, feeding off the energy of the other animals, until his cognizance descended into primitive thoughts and his body was too exhausted to move. Let the others worry about the human lass. If she was smart, she would stay in his apartment like she'd been asked. Or better yet, leave as she kept threatening.

A few hours later, Lucian slowed to an easy lope, then came to a complete stop. His breath sounded loud in his ears. Snowflakes drifted around him, landing silently in the trees and on the forest floor. The air was clean. The wind calm and still. The animals snuggled up in their beds.

His head felt heavy, and he lowered his nose to the ground, wetting the tip in the fresh snow. He had run far and hard, but that oppressed feeling had not left him, nor had the anger and frustration. He thought again about what Cedric had said, for before, in his anger and need to get away, he hadn't truly listened. But now he remembered. He wanted to talk to him about Keelin.

And tell him…what?

An uneasy feeling wormed its way into his stomach. He shook his head, then his entire body, casting off the snow. The urge to get back to Keelin, to protect her, was suddenly overwhelming. With one last look around at the magical winter forest around him, Lucian turned around and headed back the way he had come.

It was only a few hours before dawn when his large paws picked their way through the trees behind the apartments. The snow hadn't followed him off the mountains, yet the three-story building was barely visible against the dark, gray sky. There was a light on in his window and another in Cedric's, casting shadows in the trees. The humans who paid Cedric rent were all asleep. No one would see him.

Shifting back to his human form, he breathed through the pain, and when it was done, he crouched down on all fours on the cold ground, catching his breath and getting used to the feeling of being on only two legs again. The wind ruffled his hair, and the sweet scent of honey flowers filled his nose. His eyes found her right before she spoke.

"I thought you might need these." Keelin stood not ten feet away, bundled up in a heavy blue coat he rarely used, her arms full with a change of clothing for him. The coat fell nearly to her knees. Her legs were bare. Her boots were unlaced on her feet.

Lucian remained where he was, remembering what was underneath that coat, and enjoying the way her eyes traveled over his body.

When she found his face again, her cheeks were tinged red, and he could tell from her scent it wasn't from the cold. She glanced away, toward the apartments, then back. "I wasn't sure where you went, then Duncan stopped by and let me know you'd gone for a run. So, I watched for you from the window." Her eyes dropped. Came back.

She was nervous. Why?

"After a while, I got restless. I couldn't sleep. And I didn't know where to find Bronaugh. Plus it was getting late. So, I thought it would be okay if I came and sat out here to wait. Get some fresh air."

Something tugged at the edge of his memory. Something about the two females together. Something that should be obvious, and yet, he couldn't quite grasp it. The frustration that had never really left him that night began to grow, eating away at his insides until he couldn't stand being with himself. He needed a distraction, something else to focus on.

And she was standing right in front of him.

Lucian moved, a little fast if the way she sucked in a surprised breath was any indication. She blinked when he took the clothes from her arms and dropped them on the ground. "Touch me," he ground out. "Touch me, Keelin. The way ye did before."

For a few seconds, he didn't think she would. Then the coat rustled as her arm moved, and her bare fingertips skimmed over his left hipbone. All of the rage, all of the frustration, it all refocused to that one little spot of skin and how her touch made him feel. Lucian's muscles rippled along his spine, the need he felt for this female trying to redirect itself into shifting. With some effort, he fought it back, concentrating on her blue-green eyes that stared trustingly up into his.

Her other hand rose and she pressed her palm to the center of his chest. His heart began to pound, reaching for her from beneath his breastbone. Lucian wanted to crawl inside of this female. Wanted to bury himself in her until all of the destructive energy that had been eating away at him all of his life drained away in waves of desire and his body was too spent to care. All he had to do was allow himself to be lost.

Keelin touched his face. Her eyes shone in the dim light. "Lucian, I need to tell you something."

"Nay, lass. No' now." Something inside of him knew he didn't want to hear whatever it was she was about to say.

"Lucian." Her voice cracked on his name. Pleading.

He could see the struggle in the lines around her mouth and the pain in her eyes, and his heart wept.

NO. He didn't want to know what she had to say. He would listen later. But not right now. Right now, he needed to be with her.

Catching her small hands within his own, he pulled her to him and took her mouth. He kissed her until she stopped trying to talk and kissed him back, her hunger for him rising to the surface.

No. He didn't want to hear what she had to say. Not when her sweet breath mingled with his own and her nails dug into his palms. Keelin hung on to him as though she were afraid he was about to be swept away into one of the Faerie prince's warp holes.

Lucian felt the same.

He pressed kisses to her lips, her jaw, the freckles on her wee nose, the soft skin just in front of her ear. "I want ye, lass. 'n' I dinna think I can wait tae get back inside." His entire body trembled with need, his sex hard and thick and straining toward her heat. Releasing her hands, he scowled at the cold night around them.

Keelin stepped back, and he groaned aloud at the loss, thinking she was leaving him to go back inside. But then she unzipped the heavy coat she had borrowed.

She wore nothing beneath it.

Lucian lost his breath at the sight of all of that soft skin. It was enough to bring him to his knees, and indeed, he found he couldn't hold his own weight and fell to the ground in front of her. Her full hips filled his large hands, and he looked up, past the perfect curves of her breasts, to find her watching him with parted lips and eyes that danced with all of the colors of the sea. The musky scent of her sex mixed with the natural sweet honey of her skin, and Lucian groaned as he accepted the gift of seeing her naked and wanting. For him.

He ran his hands up over her rib cage to heft the weight of her breasts, the nipples hard against his palms and harder still when he plucked them. He slid them back down to her hips, and pulled her closer so he could press his lips to the soft curve of her belly. His Keelin was built like the hearty women of his homeland, both strong and soft, with thick hips and thighs and not a bone to be seen. Woman enough to take a male like him.

Sitting back on his haunches, Lucian ran his nose over the soft, reddish curls before him, breathing her in. His mouth watered at the thought of tasting her. "Spread yer legs for me, Keelin."

She shuffled her feet to the sides, leaning back against the tree trunk behind her. Lucian looked up, taking it all in one more time. Her eyes churned with color as they watched him, full of anticipation. Her breasts rose and fell with quick breaths. Her heart pounded in his sensitive ears.

He ran his tongue over his bottom lip as her scent

grew stronger, and when he leaned in and pressed it to her silky folds, she was wet and ready for him.

Though his cock ached with needs of its own, Lucian took his time, imprinting her taste on his tongue so he could remember it always. And when she came, he didn't stop, but forced her to ride it out until her knees gave way and her body fell limp and satiated. Then, and only then, did he press her back against the tree, lift her leg around his hip, and slide inside of her with a growl of pleasure.

With the coat protecting her back, he siphoned into the rage twisting his insides, letting it go, releasing it into Keelin with every thrust of his hips. She cried out in his ear, urging him on, and he pushed harder, demanding more from her, needing to hear her, needing the connection. And when he came, he locked eyes with her and brought her with him this time.

With her moans filling his ears, his upper lip lifted in a snarl as biting pleasure shot down his spine and through his balls. Keelin stiffened in his arms, crying out, her body arching, taking him deeper as she convulsed around him.

Lucian lost himself. Lost himself in this female until his bones joined with hers and their souls entwined on a kiss.

When it was over, he supported her against the tree, still inside of her, blocking the cold air with his body.

"Lucian, I need to tell you something."

No. No, Keelin.

Please.

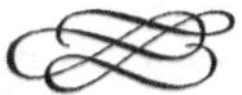

CHAPTER 18

"Lucian, I need to tell you something." He still held her against the tree, a hand beneath each leg and his face buried in the side of her throat.

"Och, Keelin. I dinnae want tae hear it. Truly, I don't." His voice was rough with a myriad of emotions.

She felt the pain running through him. All the way to her bones. It matched her own. "I wish I didn't have to." She had to stop. Get control of herself. "But you need to know who I am. You deserve to know."

With a great, heavy sigh, he pressed a hard kiss to her neck, disentangled them and set her on her feet. He pulled the coat closed around her, zipping it up and shutting out the cold air. But he couldn't shut out the icy wall rising between them.

The fight had gone out of him. He wouldn't even look at her.

"Lucian, there's something you need to know about me."

The muscles jumped in his jaw as he stared at the ground between them. "Do I, now?" There was a touch of anger in his voice. But also hurt. And a tinge of disgust. With her? Or himself?

Oh, gods. He already knows.

He looked up at her, and there was no animation in his features. His emotions were completely closed off, his eyes cold and gray as morning clouds. "Wha' is it I need tae ken?"

Keelin struggled to find words. There had to be a way to tell him that wouldn't send him running away. Or worse, end with his hands wrapped around her throat.

"Lucian, I'm—"

"Lucian," a deep voice spoke from behind him.

Keelin eyes were hot and wet with tears as she found Cedric over Lucian's bare shoulder. He stood ten yards away, invading this moment between them. Anger ran hot through her veins. "How long have you been here?"

"No' long, but just in time it sounds like." He crossed his arms over his wide chest. "Dinna worry, Keelin. I did no' see anything."

Lucian never took his eyes from her. "He's telling the truth," he told her.

She turned her attention back to the alpha. "I want to tell him myself. Alone."

But Cedric shook his head. "I cannae let ye do tha', Keelin. It's no' safe."

"He won't hurt me."

"Do ye ken tha' for sure?"

Keelin glanced back at Lucian. He hadn't moved. Hadn't acknowledged Cedric's presence. His attention was fully on her, and she suddenly felt like a hare frozen before the hunter. But it was too late. He'd already seen her for exactly what she was. The tears spilled over. "No," she whispered. "I don't."

Cedric held out his arm, keeping one eye on Lucian. "Come here, lass."

Heart splitting within her chest, she did as he told her.

"Lucian," Cedric's voice had dropped, and even Keelin felt the need to drop to her knees before him. "Get yer clothes on."

Lucian turned. "Just tell me wha' it is I need tae ken." He crossed his arms over his chest, standing proud and nude before them. He sneered at Cedric. "Actually, ye dinna have tae. I ken what she is, Cedric. Though, I dinna want tae admit it tae myself until just now. And, o' course, no one bothered tae fucking tell me any different." His eyes shifted to her briefly, and the way he looked at her shattered the broken pieces of her heart. "She is Fae. I ken tha'. What I dinna ken is what side she is on. No' tha' it matters much. At least no' tae me."

Keelin wanted to go to him. To take the pain away. Because that's exactly what this was. Pain. Not anger. Not bigotry. But pain. It was the pain of a little boy who'd seen his entire village killed. The pain of a man who could never kill enough to avenge them, and was no longer allowed to. "Lucian…" Whatever she was about to say was lost when those icy eyes bore right through her. There wasn't a trace of kindness or understanding in them.

"Keelin is very important tae us, lad. She is no' *na maithe* or *an olc*, but both. As was her mother before her."

Keelin saw it on Lucian's face the moment under-standing dawned.

Cedric placed a large hand on her shoulder. "Keelin is The Key, Lucian. She will save us all. 'n' ye need tae be on board with tha'."

Lucian eyes shot to the place where Cedric touched her, and a deep growl filled the air. Her core filled with hope. If he cared enough to threaten his alpha, then maybe all was not lost. But that hope was quickly dashed by his next words.

"So, this was all planned out from the verra start." He released a bark of laughter that held no humor. "This was why no one else could watch the lass, but me. Ye wanted this!" He waved his hand back and forth between himself and Keelin. Then he looked skyward, the smile on his face not a smile at all, but something much more sinister. "Wha' did ye think would happen, Cedric? Did ye think I would fuck her and her magic cunt would sway me tae be like ye and Marc and Brock?"

Keelin felt her cheeks heat, but it was more from anger than embarrassment. Cedric stepped forward, but she held up a hand to stop him.

She lifted her chin. "You sure thought my cunt was magical just a few minutes ago."

Cold, gray eyes shifted to her. "Fuck *ye*, Keelin."

Cedric was in his face before he finished saying her name. "Apologize tae the lass, pup."

"I will no'," Lucian gritted through his teeth. Arms at his sides, he visibly strained against Cedric's will. "'n' fuck ye, too."

Growls filled the air as the two males faced each other.

The skin on Lucian's arms and legs rippled as the muscle beneath shifted. "I will no' be led around by my cock like ye, Cedric. I ken wha' these things are like. Ye can no' trust them."

Things? Now she was a thing?

The two males were circling each other now.

"I am your alpha, Lucian. I decide wha' is good or no' good for this pack. 'n' I'm getting right tired o' always having tae remind ye o' tha' fact."

"Maybe ye dinna need tae be my alpha anymore." He spit on the ground at Cedric's feet.

In an explosion of breaking bones and tearing muscle, the two males shifted. Lucian finished first, and went right for Cedric's throat. But he was knocked aside when the alpha threw his weight into him, jaws snapping shut an inch from Lucian's muzzle.

Keelin didn't know what to do. She stood to the side, wringing her hands, as the two males growled and snarled, yipping in pain when someone managed to get their teeth into the other.

Cedric was larger, his black fur thick, his eyes glowing white. He fought with a cool head, anticipating every move Lucian made. And as the fight wore on, Lucian got more and more reckless.

"There's nothing ye can do, lass. It's our way. Ye have tae let them fight it out."

Keelin turned away from the fight to find she was surrounded by wolves. Duncan was the one who had spoke. He was accompanied by a male with short, dark hair and another with long, wavy brown hair and a short beard. The longhaired male watched the fight with blue eyes full of anxiety and regret. None of them tried to interfere.

Keelin tried to get through to them. "Lucian won't win. Cedric will kill him! You can't just stand there and watch it happen."

"Aye, lass. We can."

"And we will. It's against the laws o' the pack tae get in the middle o' a fight."

Keelin knew this. And yet to see it playing out first hand in front of her eyes, with the challenger being a male she cared about, was something else entirely. Lucian had been cruel to her just now, but it was only because he was hurting, and rightly so. She'd lied to him. Hidden her identity from him. As had the rest of his pack. The only family he knew. Of course he felt betrayed. Hurt. And the way Lucian dealt with hurt was to get angry. He probably felt like he'd lost his family all over again. Or that they'd never really accepted him to begin with.

She couldn't just stand here and let him be killed. Because she knew he wouldn't submit. No. He would rather Cedric kill him than have it proven he was the weaker wolf.

The two wolves broke apart with a snap of jaws and a spray of blood, and Keelin saw her chance and took it. Running out into the middle of the fight with all of the speed she was blessed with, she threw herself in front of Lucian.

Cedric caught himself mid-lunge, his huge front paws landing just to the side of her feet and his teeth tearing into the air beside her face. In the pre-dawn light, Keelin saw his muzzle dripped with blood. His feet on the ground, he lowered his head and snarled. Long, sharp teeth not an inch from her nose. Heart pounding, she stood her ground, and after a few tense seconds, the alpha backed off a few steps.

Her lungs began to ache and Keelin realized she'd been holding her breath. The cold air burned her lungs as she breathed deep once. Then again. She began to shake, whether it was from the cold or her brush with death, she couldn't say.

She'd taken a huge chance, counting on the fact Cedric wouldn't hurt her because she was too important to him. To the world.

Lucian's huge head came up alongside her and he knocked her out of the way. Keelin landed hard on her side and jumped right back to her feet. He had wounds in his shoulder and the side of his throat. His breath wheezed in his lungs. And when he shifted his weight to growl at her, she saw he was favoring his front left leg.

There was no chance in hell he would survive this fight. Not without her interference.

Cedric came up behind her, snapping his teeth, little growls telling her to get out of the way. When she didn't listen, he looked over his shoulder at the rest of the pack.

The three males came forward to remove her, their expressions wary but set.

Reaching deep for powers she hadn't used in many years, Keelin delved into their minds and, with a softly spoken order, bid them to stay where they were. When they were restrained, she turned to Cedric. "I'm sorry. I cannot let you kill him. Let him go."

The large, black wolf began to pace back and forth

before her. One eye on Lucian as though he were trying to find a way around her.

Keelin was not a tiny female, but even she, with all her Fae magic, felt cowed in the path of this wolf. She could show no fear. "I will take you out if I have to. Please don't make me do that, Cedric. You're the most respected alpha of all the packs. It would be a huge loss to everyone involved to lose you. But I'll do it if it means saving Lucian." She risked a glance at the snarling wolf beside her. His glowing gray eyes had never left her face. But though he threatened, she was heartened to see he had yet to try to hurt her.

Cedric paced, clearly weighing out his options. Tense minutes ticked by. Keelin ignored the angry males of the pack as they tried to convince her she was interfering where she shouldn't and to let them go. She also ignored Lucian, who was telling her the same thing with every trick of intimidation he knew other than hurting her outright. Finally, she went to place a hand on his head to calm him. Lucian leapt away before she could touch him, upper lip lifted in an angry snarl.

Keelin pushed aside the pain his actions caused and turned back to Cedric. She concentrated on the alpha. No matter what, Lucian—as of this moment—was still a member of his pack. If Cedric wouldn't fight him, he would obey whatever decision his alpha made until the challenge could be acted upon. It was the law of the packs.

At least she hoped he would obey. If not, she would have to take further action. Neither wolf would appreciate it. Lucian would downright hate her for sure. But she would not, could not, let him die.

Finally, Cedric stopped his pacing and stared at Keelin with white, glowing eyes. They moved to Lucian, and with obvious intention, the large wolf turned his back and sat.

The fight for dominance wasn't over, but it was postponed. For now.

Keelin turned to Lucian. The fur on his back was raised in anger, his teeth were bared, and blood dripped from his wounds. He might never forgive her for this. "I'm sorry," she told him. His angry visage blurred as tears filled her eyes. "I couldn't let you die, Lucian. I know you hate me. And I can live with that. For now. As long as I know you're alive out there somewhere."

He leaned forward on his good leg and shoved his muzzle right into her face, teeth bared. For a brief moment, her heart stopped.

Then, he spun on his back paws and limped into the forest.

Without so much as a glance, Cedric walked away in the opposite direction, his gait stiff. She waited long enough for tempers to cool, and then she released the others.

The rest of the pack surrounded her, cutting off her view of Lucian as the trees swallowed him before ushering her back inside. She stayed with Bronaugh and Marc all day and all night.

When she awoke, she found out Lucian had come home, packed a few of his things, and left.

CHAPTER 19

Lucian checked his phone. There was a text message he'd almost forgotten about. It had come in the night before as he was checking into the Red Lion Hotel in Cheyenne, but it was from a number he didn't know and he'd been too crabbit to read it. Instead, the phone had ended up on the desk with his keys while he took a shower and treated his wounds. Afterward, he'd tried to get some sleep, but even after driving seventeen-plus hours straight, he couldn't settle. So, he'd walked down the road a bit and gotten some tacos.

The ride from Washington to Wyoming had done little to calm the renewed rage and embarrassment rolling around inside of him. At one point, he'd nearly stopped the car so he could shift and travel off-road. The only thing that had stopped him was knowing it would be a wee bit difficult getting new clothes when he arrived at wherever he was going. The locals were sure to raise a fuss if he went waltzing into the nearest Wal-Mart bare-arsed and with no money to pay.

A part of him was tempted to do it, and not shift back. Ever. He preferred the simple freedom of his wolf over life as a human, anyway. But running wild as a wolf/man had its own risks. The most likely being getting himself shot by an over-exuberant hunter.

The second reason, well, he couldn't examine the second reason too closely. Not just yet. Maybe in time.

The thought had crossed his mind to go to Texas and see if Keegan would take him in, but Lucian dismissed it almost immediately. That Fae-loving pack was no better than this one ever since the southern Alpha had decided he'd rather fuck Faeries then use them as the gods intended—as entertainment.

So, he'd just kept driving.

After Keelin had interfered with his challenge to Cedric, he'd run the mountains all night until he'd calmed enough to shift back. When he'd returned to get his things, he hadn't expected anyone to stop him back at the apartments, and they hadn't. As a matter of fact, the rest of his pack had been suspiciously out of sight. They were giving him space to leave with what little dignity he had left. Not even Duncan was waiting to smirk at him and offer whatever unsolicited advice he decided to spout off. At the time, Lucian had been too angry to appreciate what they'd done. But he did now, sitting alone in his hotel room with only his own thoughts for company.

Unsurprisingly, Keelin hadn't been at his place when he'd gone back. Whether the pack had moved her or she'd moved herself, he didn't know. But without him there to "protect" her, it made sense she had to be with someone who could.

Probably Duncan, the bastard.

Lucian bared his teeth at the thought. Even now. After all the lies. He wanted her.

His phone lit up with a new message, and Lucian tapped the screen.

HEY, Lucian. It's Sara. Did you get my message? I was wondering if we could meet? I'm in the States.

ANOTHER MESSAGE CAME in right after it.

PLEASE, Lucian. I have something very important to tell you. Something I should've told you a long time ago. Call me at this number -Sara

HE ALMOST IGNORED THE MESSAGES. He hadn't seen Sara since she'd appeared with his old alpha after Brock had come back from never-never land. And before that it had been a good four years since he'd left their old pack in Scotland...

After Brock took the fall for him and was banished from their territory.

Because of Sara.

Lucian hit the call back button and put the phone to his ear. As he waited for it to go through, he glanced around the light and airy room as though seeing it for the first time. The place actually wasn't too bad.

Sara picked up on the first ring. "Lucian…"

"How did ye get this number?" He wasn't sure how he'd feel when he heard her voice again. It was curiosity more than anything else that had driven his decision to call her. But with one word—his name—she'd answered that burning question.

Nothing.

He felt nothing at all.

"I got it from Brock."

The bloody bastard. If he ever saw his old friend again he'd punch him in that blathering mouth of his. "What do ye want, Sara?"

"Can ye meet me?"

"I'm no' in Seattle."

"I ken that. Yer at the Red Lion Hotel." A pause. "So am I." Another pause. "I saw what happened with ye 'n' Cedric. I'd just gotten tae yer place 'n' heard a ruckus around back, so I walked around. I saw everything. After ye ran off, I went back tae my car. I was going tae leave, but I decided tae hang around 'n' see if ye came back. When ye did, I followed ye here."

Lucian felt his cheeks burn with embarrassment that she had seen his humiliation. Sure enough, she would spread the word far and wide. "Ye followed me across the bloody country?"

"Technically, it was only halfway, or thereabouts." Her laugh was strained. "We need tae talk, Lucian."

Well, why the fuck not? He didn't have much to lose at this point. And he doubted she would've gone through all of this trouble if it weren't important. "Meet me in the fitness center. It's sure tae be empty."

"I could come tae yer room?" she said a little too quickly.

"No. The fitness center." He hung up the call.

She was waiting for him when he got there, sitting on a weight bench, and she looked just the same as the last time he'd seen her. Maybe her dark hair was a wee bit shorter.

She stood when he entered.

Lucian glanced around. "Where is Finn?"

"He's back home, with Thomas."

"Ye left yer son with yer alpha? What about his father?"

She looked down at her hands, twisted in front of her hips. "That's what I'm here tae talk tae ye about, Lucian." Taking a deep breath, she looked him right in the eye. "*You* are Finn's da, Lucian. And I'm here tae ask ye tae come home, back tae Scotland, 'n' be a part o' his life. Ye dinna have tae be with me, if ye dinna want tae, but it's no' right o' me tae have kept this hidden from ye all these years. Yer son is almost eleven. He needs his da. His real da." She stopped. Took a breath. "It's time ye both knew the truth."

Many thoughts and emotions went through Lucian as she spoke, none of which made the least bit of sense. "Dinna fuck with me, Sara. I'm no' in the mood."

"I'm telling the truth, Lucian."

Something fluttered inside his stomach. Could it be true?

He studied her expression. No, she was spinning tales. If what she said was true, why would she only be telling him this now? Sara always put her own self first and foremost. Sure, she must have her reasons for telling him something like this, but it wasn't because of any lingering feelings of guilt. "Finn looks nothing like me."

"He has yer light locks, like ye did when ye were younger, before they darkened with the fire ye have in there now."

"That doesn't prove he is mine."

"I'm no' lying tae ye, Lucian." She came toward him, her hands up in a pleading gesture. "When I found out I was pregnant, I was scared. Everything was so tense, especially in my home. I was feart for my life if I told anyone the child wasn't Jaime's. He'd just taken me back."

"And now? Does he ken now?"

She looked down at the concrete floor between them and shook her head. "No, and he can no' ever ken."

Lucian stared at her. It was hard to believe he had once cared so much about this female he had risked his own arse, and the only true friend he'd ever really had, for her. "Ye want me tae come back tae Scotland, 'n' watch another male raise the child ye claim is mine?"

She bit her lower lip, pleading at him with her eyes. "I ken it's no' ideal, but—"

"No' ideal??" He barked out a laugh. "No' ideal, she says."

"But ye could be a part o' his life. And, ye would have a pack tae come home tae." She hurried on. "Do ye think Thomas will take ye back if he finds out the truth? Or finds out what just happened with ye 'n' Cedric? 'n' where else are ye gonna go? Are ye going tae be a *siubhal*? Ye wouldn't make it as a lone wolf, Lucian."

"Brock survived just fine on his own."

"Brock got damn lucky, 'n' ye ken that's all it was." She crossed her arms, and a look that was dangerously smug overtook the nervous expression she'd worn since he'd entered the gym. "Besides, by wha' I heard and saw in those woods, I think ye will find our pack much more tae yer taste these days."

He rubbed the back of his neck. He was tired. And he was angry. And he just wanted to be alone. But...a child. Could it be? Was he a da?

She stepped closer, her expression willing him to listen. "Thomas is no' like Cedric, Lucian. He believes in the old ways. 'n' the old ways dinna involve diluting our packs or sacrificing our numbers. Wolves need tae stick with our own kind. It's no' natural tae be mating with things like Faeries. Thomas believes what's happening in Seattle 'n' Texas is all part o' Prince Nada's grand plan, tae wither away our numbers by sending Faeries tae seduce our wolves and reduce the number o' our offspring." She searched his face. "It makes perfect sense, Lucian. Think about it. The prince has been traveling the earth visiting wolf packs, making promises, giving them things, so we will owe him 'n' help him beat the Dark Fae. 'n' while he did that, he saw an opportunity, 'n' he sent his Faeries tae seduce our wolves. Tae mate with them. Wolves 'n' Faeries can no' make babies. The more Fae tha' mate with our wolves, the less wolves there will be."

Lucian pulled his mind away from thoughts of possible fatherhood long enough to think about what she was saying. To really think about it. Sara was right. It made perfect sense. The Fae could not be trusted. He'd always known this, and now he had proof.

Keelin's hesitant touch and trusting aqua eyes washed through him. His head jerked toward the doorway, convinced for a moment he'd smelled honey flowers. But no, it was gone. The scent was only in his head, as was the memory of her.

He forced himself to focus on Sara. The lure of a pack wasn't enough to sway him, but the promise of a child…a son…would he be able to live a life as the lad's uncle?

For now. Perhaps. Until he got to the bottom of the question of Finn's parentage.

"I'll come with ye, Sara. But only for Finn. 'n' I will do as ye ask. I will no' tell anyone what ye told me about him being mine. I'll continue tae be his 'uncle' as I was before I left."

She smiled up at him, but her eyes were sad. She couldn't possibly want to be with him after all this time? No, he didn't get that feeling from her. The melancholy was for a different reason. "Good, because I already bought your ticket. We leave late tonight. I have a cab coming to take us to the airport at ten."

Lucian nodded.

Sara put her hands on his shoulder and pulled him down to kiss him on the cheek. Just like she used to. But the kiss was awkward. Her touch cold. Her scent all wrong. She backed away, giving him a knowing smile. "I'm glad yer joining us. We need all the help we can get if we're going tae take out the prince 'n' all o' his Faeries."

Lucian called after her as she headed to the door. "What do ye mean, take out his Faeries?"

She stopped with one hand on the door handle. "We're going tae kill them, Lucian. All o' them. Thomas is gathering all o' the like-minded packs together. We're waging a war o' our own. And we won't stop until every last Faerie is dead. No' just the *an olc*." Her smile was real this time as she pulled open the door. "See ye tonight."

When she was gone. Lucian took her spot on the weight bench and put his head in his hands. A da. He was a da. Well, possibly. He was going back to Scotland. Tonight. Thomas would take him back. He needed every wolf he could get. To wage war against the Fae. All of the Fae. Against Brock's Heather. And Marc's Bronaugh.

Against his Keelin.

Lucian reached for the anger that had fueled him all this way, but all he found was numbness. No, not numb. Empty. He felt empty. Like he had a giant hole inside of him. The lass had made a fool of him in front of his pack. She had caused him to dishonor his alpha by stopping the fight. But now, alone with Sara's words and without the poison of his anger distracting him, he knew why she had done it. She had told him as much. And if he were to be honest with himself, he would've done the same. If the tables had been turned, he could not have stood by and watched her die.

And he wasn't going to do so now.

Lucian got up and strode to the door. He was going to the airport all right, but it wasn't to fly to Scotland. He was going home. To his true home. Cedric may very well insist they finish what they started, but he would hear him out first. Lucian would make him by whatever means he had. Seeing Sara again had made one thing perfectly clear —child or no child, she was not his family. Family stuck by each other, no matter what. Family sacrificed for each other. Family put up with each other even when they were being right bastards. Family loved each other enough to protect each other, even if it fucked up your own life in the process.

Family didn't care if you were wolf or Fae or anything in between.

Cedric would not join Thomas's cause. Lucian knew his alpha well enough to know this. And if Cedric and his pack were in the way, he would be taken down, as would the others who were only doing as their alpha commanded. Cedric, Marc, Duncan…

He would lose Brock.

He would lose Keelin.

Lucian hastened his steps until he was nearly running back to his hotel room. *No.* He would not stand idle and let others take the fall because he was too full of self-righteous anger aimed at all the wrong people. Not again. This time he would be a male, not a child. He would fight for his brother and his female.

My female.

Aye. Keelin was his. And it was high time his crabbit arse learned to accept that fact.

CHAPTER 20

"Keelin! Ye cannae go running off like this. No' now. I'm sorry, lass, but I can no' allow it." Cedric stood off to the side with his arms crossed over his chest and a very stern look on his handsome face.

Keelin thanked Bronaugh for the heavy shirt and coat she'd loaned her, then again refused her offer of a car. The fact that the vehicle Bronaugh was trying to loan out wasn't hers didn't seem to deter her in the least from offering to loan it out, but Keelin told her she was more comfortable getting her own vehicle. Duncan, Marc and Brock had been running patrols overnight, and Duncan had just checked in to let Cedric know they'd seen no signs of soul suckers between here and Keelin's house in Darrington.

With a quick hug for her new friend and a promise to check in as soon as she found her errant werewolf, Keelin strolled toward the door in her newly borrowed, better fitting jacket and muddy boots. She'd sat around this place for two days waiting to hear some word on Lucian. She was done waiting.

Cedric stopped her before she could leave. "Keelin, ye cannae go out there. It's no' safe."

She sighed and turned around. "I have to, Cedric. I can't let Lucian just...*leave* like this. And you shouldn't either."

He had the decency to look distressed for a moment, but then he threw his shoulders back and lifted his chin. "The lad made his choice when he challenged his alpha. Ye should no' have interfered. If anyone is responsible for Lucian running off the way he did, it's ye."

Keelin couldn't believe he was trying to lay this on her. "If I hadn't interfered, you would've killed him!" She poked him in the chest. "One of your own pack!"

"Aye!" Cedric leaned down until they were nose to nose. "I would have if the pup had pushed me tae it! No' because I wanted tae, but because tha' is our way. It's pack law. And tha' pup has pushed me more times than I care tae count. If I'd let him off easy, he wouldn't respect himself or me. And neither would the rest o' my pack."

"Maybe if you stopped calling that grown male a 'pup', he would be more apt to work with you."

"If Lucian wants me tae stop calling him a pup, he should no' act like one!"

Bronaugh came over and held her hands up between them. "You know, she has a point, Cedric."

Straightening up until he was towering over both females, Cedric dropped his head back and sighed. "Aye, I pushed Lucian." He raised his head. "As did Duncan. But it was for his own good. The pup—" He paused. "The male needed tae learn tae control his temper, for his own safety 'n' that o' the pack. Pushing his buttons the way we do, there's a good reason for it." Reaching over his shoulder, he pulled out the hairband holding his long hair back, smoothed his ponytail, and refastened it. "Och. Why did I ever think it a good idea tae allow yer kind into our midst?"

Keelin and Bronaugh exchanged a look and Bronaugh said, "I know you're not talking shit about us being Faeries."

Cedric barked out a laugh. "Ha! No, lass. I'm talking about ye being females!"

Keelin stuck her finger in his chest again to get his attention. "I'm going after Lucian. And when I bring him back here, you have to promise not to kill him. Because if you do, I won't help you. Do you hear me? I won't help any of you."

"Och, lass. Ye cannae go around saying things like that. It would be the end o' the world, 'n' well ye ken it!"

Blue energy sparked from her fingertips. "I can, and I will."

Cedric's eyes went wide and he rubbed his arms like he could feel the electricity, but he didn't promise. "I can no', Keelin. I'm sorry."

Bronaugh came to stand closer to her, and when Keelin glanced at her, Bronaugh smiled, her eyes a beautiful rainbow of colors. They did nothing but stand there. However, without a spoken word between them, their Fae magic swirled in the air. Outside, thunder rumbled and the wind picked up, brushing tree branches across the window.

Taking a step back, Cedric crossed himself. "Och, aye! All right! I promise! I promise I will no' kill Lucian!"

Keelin lowered her hands and Bronaugh stepped off to the side. The light drizzle of winter rain hitting the windows was the only sound. "And you'll let him back into the pack."

Icy cold eyes narrowed in on her, but Keelin would not back down. If she was going to stay with these wolves, the only way she would do it was with Lucian at her side. "Promise me, wolf."

"If Lucian wants tae come back, he can fight his way back in tae the pack. But I'm no' just letting him getting away with wha' he did like nothing happened."

Keelin gave him a sharp nod. "That's fair." Giving Bronaugh a quick hug, she turned to go.

"If ye insist on going, I'm escorting ye tae yer house," Cedric told her. "I insist. If anything happened tae ye…" His expression became quite grave. "It would no' be good."

"No," Keelin said. "It wouldn't. Which is why I'm going alone."

"Keelin—"

"The world will need you Cedric. But let's hope that doesn't happen." With a grin, she blew him a kiss and was outside before he could stop her again. She breathed in deep. The night was cold and still and had the bite of snow on the air.

Now, to go get her wolf.

CHAPTER 21

The trip back to Seattle took five hundred and seventy years. By the time the plane landed, Lucian was about ready to bust out of his skin. But then again, he could've traveled home at the speed of light and it wouldn't have been fast enough to suit him.

Sara would know he had checked out of the hotel by now. Hopefully, she would let him get a head start before she told Thomas their plan had failed, if for no other reason than they used to mean something to each other. Whatever that something was. And, quite possibly, had a child together.

The thought still blew Lucian's mind. And he would get to the bottom of what she'd told him, come hell or high water, just as soon as he could. But for now, Finn was safe with his mam. Sara was many things—some of them better than others—but she was a ferocious mother. She would protect the lad with her dying breath, and do what needed to be done to ensure his well-being. Lucian had no doubt of that. And pups were cherished and protected by the entire pack. No one would hurt the lad before Lucian could figure out if he was truly his da or not.

Though it would've been faster to run back to the pack's apartment building, a giant wolf speeding through the city of Seattle would cause a wee bit too much notice, so Lucian settled on renting a car. Luckily, it was late enough that traffic was thinning out.

His stomach tightened as he pulled into the apartment parking lot. He had no idea what kind of reception would be waiting for him. As far as he knew, a fight for dominance of a pack had never ended with both parties still alive. So his coming back was sure to be uncomfortable, if not fatal. And that was fine. He deserved whatever Cedric decided to do. His temper had caused him to make a rash decision, again, and he would accept the consequences.

He just needed to make Cedric listen to him first, then he would be happy to take whatever was coming for him once he knew Keelin and his pack were safe.

Shutting off the rental car, Lucian got out and walked cautiously to the front door in full view of the security cameras.

Duncan met him at the top of the stairs. His green eyes traveled over Lucian, gauging his mood. "What are ye doing here, Lucian?"

"I need tae speak tae Cedric." He paused. Cleared his throat. "And Keelin. It's verra important." Lucian didn't want to say anything else until he had Cedric in front of him.

For a moment, he didn't think Duncan was going to let him pass. But then he stepped aside and let him go. Arms crossed over his chest, he gave Lucian a good deal of side-eye. "Yer lucky ye weren't taken out the moment ye landed in Seattle."

Lucian turned to him in surprise.

"Brock is at the airport. Sara called him looking for ye. Told him some kind o' tale about ye comin' back tae take Cedric out when he wasn't expecting it, 'n' how she tried tae talk ye out o' it. He was going tae try tae stop ye. But then saw ye getting off a plane."

The fucking bitch. Lucian decided right then and there if the boy was truly his, he would do whatever he needed to do to bring him back with him. "Why didn't he say anything tae me?"

Duncan shrugged. "Guess he wanted tae see what ye would do." The door opened and he stepped inside. "Come on, then. I take it yer no' here tae do anything dishonorable being tha' ye walked right up tae the front door, bold as can be."

When they got to Cedric's place, the door was open and the alpha was sitting in his favorite armchair, beer in one hand, and the other gripping the arm of the chair.

The determination that had brought Lucian this far drained out of him when he met the detached, icy-blue eyes of his alpha. For the first time in his life, he took up a submissive posture without being forced into it. Eyes on Cedric's large, boot-covered feet, Lucian kept his voice level as he spoke. "I have something verra important tae tell ye, Cedric. All I ask is that ye hear me out before ye react tae my coming back here."

There was silence as he waited for the alpha's decision. He very well could have just told him everything, forced him to listen, but Lucian figured he owed Cedric better than that after all the trouble he'd caused him over the years. He'd had a lot of time to think on the flight back here, and Lucian had admitted to himself he'd been lashing out at the wrong person all this time. He'd blamed Cedric for not being allowed to take revenge on the ones who had killed his family when he was a child. Blamed Cedric for his feelings of helplessness. And Cedric had taken the brunt of all of that anger.

But what he had never permitted himself to acknowledge was that Cedric had lost loved ones to the Fae, too. They all had. If not during the war, then after, before Prince Nada started bringing the two species together. And Keelin had opened his eyes even more. His feelings for her were not wrong. Something Brock and Marc already knew, as did Keegan, the Texas alpha. And if *that* wolf could win over the Faerie lass of his dreams, there was hope for Lucian as well.

A great sigh filled the space between them. "I have a question for ye first, Lucian."

Lucian glanced up in confusion. "Aye?"

"Yer fiery temper aside, do ye want tae stay in this pack, or no?"

Was he offering him a chance to stay? After what he'd done? "Aye, Cedric. I would like tha' verra much."

"Then sit down 'n' say yer piece, 'n' afterward, ye will have yer chance." He took a big swallow of his beer and put the empty bottle down on the coffee table. "Duncan, grab us all a Guinness, if ye will."

"I think ye should call Marc and Brock. They should hear this, too."

"Marc is running patrols and Brock is on his way home. I can fill them in when they get here."

"I", not "we".

Lucian sat and accepted the bottle from Duncan with thanks. He took a good, long swig to brace his nerves. "I want tae apologize for dishonoring ye the way I did a few nights ago. I am no' a male who backs down from a fight, especially when I instigate it. But I could no' hurt Keelin." He took another drink. "I needed tae leave before I did anything I would truly regret. I am not trying tae excuse my behavior," he was quick to add. "I only want ye tae ken why I ran the way I did. Why I always run the way I do." The last was embarrassing to admit, but needed to be said. "I've been acting like a child, blaming everyone and everything for the pain I've carried inside ever since Brock 'n' I found our family littered about our village as kids, 'n' it's time I stop." He met Cedric's eyes. "I should've died a few nights ago. I'm no match for ye, Cedric, and I ken that, too. I will accept whatever ye decide I owe ye. But this once, I'm glad for my temper, for if I hadn't run off the way I had, I would never have found out what Thomas, my old alpha, is planning."

"Wha' is it Thomas is planning?" Cedric asked.

Lucian relayed all that happened with Sara and what she had told him. "I ken ye would no' agree with what he was planning tae do, so I came tae warn ye."

Duncan sat back against the cushions of the sofa. "Och. It's good Marc and Brock are no' here. They'd be halfway tae Scotland after hearing Thomas was threatening their females."

"Aye," Cedric said. "With good reason." He fell quiet,

but his eyes were sharp, and Lucian could practically hear that keen mind of his making a plan of action.

Lucian finished his beer and stood. "If ye dinna mind, I would like tae go speak with Keelin. There are things tha' need tae be said."

Cedric frowned as he stood also. "Keelin is no' here, Lucian."

"Where the hell is she, then?"

"She said she was going tae find *ye*," Duncan told him with a grin.

"'n' ye did no' stop her?"

"I tried," Cedric told him. "But she 'n' Bronaugh threatened me with their magic." He shuttered. "Ye ken I could do nothing tae stop her."

All three werewolves crossed themselves.

"Aye," Lucian said. "How could ye?" He turned to leave.

"She said she was going back tae her place tae get her car if tha' helps," Cedric called after him.

"Thank ye, Cedric," Lucian told him earnestly.

"Ye say what needs tae be said tae yer female, 'n' be back here tomorrow when the moon is high in the sky 'n' we'll settle things between us."

With a grave nod, Lucian let himself out.

In the woods behind the apartment building, he stripped, stored his clothes in the shelter of a tree where a couple of branches crisscrossed, and shifted. Shaking off the last vestiges of the change, he began to run.

High in the mountains, snow began to fall, but this time Lucian didn't stop to enjoy the peace of the scenery around him. He didn't stop to rest. He didn't think about what he was going to say when he got there or what he would do if Keelin wasn't still there.

At the top of the rise overlooking her house, he searched for any sign of her. Her house was dark. There was no movement. She was gone, and it could take him a long time to find her.

The truth was, it was very likely the Fae would find her first.

Pain pierced his soul. Lucian sat back on his haunches, raised his muzzle and howled his grief to the night sky. Answering howls filled the night, some close, some miles away. Coyote commiserating with his troubles. Lucian hung his head, wondering where to go now.

A light came on below, and the back door of Keelin's house opened. His lass came outside and stood in the glow coming through the window.

Lucian howled again, this time with relief, and launched himself over the edge. Slipping and sliding down the mountain, he dodged trees and rocks, skidding to an ungraceful stop when he reached the bottom. Gaining his footing, he trotted across the expanse of grass, looking right and left for anyone who wasn't in their beds. But even if there were a human neighbor up and around, they wouldn't be able to see him this far away. Not without help. And lucky for him, the night was cloudy and dark.

"Lucian?"

The disbelief in her voice egged him on, and he broke into a loping run. But when he reached the porch steps, he stopped.

She approached the stairs. "Are you okay? I was just coming to find you."

He should be angry with her for leaving the safety of the pack, and he was.

"Let me get you a blanket or something." She hurried back into the house.

Closing his eyes, Lucian shifted. He was inside the house when she came back, a soft-looking lavender comforter in her arms. Gods, she'd grown even bonnier in the short time he'd been gone.

She stopped a few feet away, her eyes roving over his nude form. His body reacted to her nearness, hardening for her, showing her how much he wanted her. But the rest of him was still wary, despite the conclusions he'd come to and how he'd missed her. This female was not who she had let on to be. Lucian felt as though he barely knew her.

Her lips parted and her eyes flared wide at the evidence of his desire. Before he could say anything, her eyes flew to his face and she spoke. "I'm so sorry for inter-fering the other night. I know how…humiliating that must have been for you. But I would do it again if it meant keeping you alive."

"Ye dinna sound verra sorry," Lucian told her.

"Well, that's because I'm not," she answered with a small smile. She took a step toward him.

He stepped back, and cursed himself when he saw the wave of hurt cross her face. "Yer a Faerie," he said by way of explanation.

"I am," she said quietly. "And I'm sorry I didn't tell you."

"This time ye sound like ye mean it."

"I do," she told him.

Och. Lucian wanted her. That much was true. But now

that he was near her again, his feelings were so mixed up. Anger, fear, hope, and loss all ran rampant inside of him.

She remained standing where she was, still wearing her boots and jacket and holding the comforter in her arms. "Lucian?"

"Aye?"

"Do you think you can ever get over what I am?"

"I would like tae try, lass." She took a step toward him and he forced himself to stay where he was. She seemed hesitant to come closer. "My soul aches for ye, Keelin. But other parts o' me are not so trusting."

Her eyes dropped to his cock. "What about that part? Does that part want to be with me?"

"Aye," he growled. "Verra much so."

"That's good," she said. "Because I was afraid I'd never see you again, and I want nothing more than to feel you inside of me right now. And maybe if we do that, the rest of you will catch up."

He gave her a nod. "I would be willing tae try."

"We might have to do it a lot."

"Aye, I would think so."

She smiled, and the joy on her face lit up the room, and his heart.

He felt an answering smile lift the corners of his mouth.

Keelin spread the comforter out right there on the open kitchen floor. With lightening speed, she ripped off her coat and boots, not bothering to hide her true nature anymore. Her hands were on the fastening of her jeans when he stopped her.

"Keelin, stop."

She froze, her expression at once confused and disappointed.

Lucian closed the distance between them. "I want tae unwrap ye myself, like a gift. Because that's what ye are tae me, lass. A gift from the gods tae calm the angry beast inside o' me. I only need tae learn tae accept it." Her scent rose strong between them, and he inhaled deep until he could taste her in the back of his throat. "Honey flowers," he murmured. Gently, he ran the back of his fingers across her cheek, over her collarbone, and down the curve of one breast. "Ye smell like honey flowers from my homeland."

"I do?" Her voice was breathless, and her chest rose and fell on quick breaths beneath his fingers.

"Aye. And now ye smell like honey flowers after a heavy rain." He met her eyes, watching the colors of the ocean swell and ebb inside of the bright orbs. Why had he never noticed the way her eyes swirled with colors? Not as brightly as Bronaugh's, but still there all the same.

But he knew why. It had been there all along, just like her scent, he just hadn't wanted to see it.

Her fingertips grazed the front of his thigh, and his breath caught. Any hesitance he felt was quickly dissipating. Gripping the bottom of the heavy shirt she wore, he lifted it up and off. She wore no undergarment, and her breasts hung heavy and full, the nipples peaking out from between her long, strawberry locks. He brushed one tip with his palm, then undid her jeans, pushing them down over her full hips and thighs. Lucian dropped to one knee to pull them from her legs, and pressed a kiss to the soft skin of her belly just above the soft curls on his way back up.

Keelin moaned, and he swelled so tight he was quite sure he would bust from his skin.

Her legs trembled as they tried to hold her weight. He kissed her *there*, and she had to catch herself on his shoulders. "Lucian…"

He rose to his full height. She trailed her fingers over the ridges of muscle covering his stomach. His skin was as pale as hers.

Her eyes dropped to his sex, and before he knew what she was about, she lowered herself until his cock was at a level with her mouth.

Lucian cupped her head in his palms, holding her still. "Keelin…"

Her eyes traveled over him. The muscles of his stomach flexed and released in anticipation, and his chest rose and fell on a shuddering breath.

She looked up at him with eyes shining with tears. "Let me touch you, Lucian. It's okay."

He clenched his teeth, but gave her a hard nod.

Keeping her eyes locked on his, she ran the tip of her tongue over him, tasting his sex. Her tongue was hot, almost feverish, on his flesh.

Keelin moaned and took him deeper into her mouth.

He pushed his hands into her hair, holding it back from her face. A low growl rumbled through his chest and throat and a shot of desire clenched his stomach. She quickly learned what he liked, and in no time at all had pushed him to the brink.

Lucian's head fell back on his shoulders and his hips

picked up her pace. One hand wrapped around the base of his cock as Keelin took him deep into her mouth, running her tongue over every inch she could find when she released him, before taking him inside again.

"Gods!" The word exploded from him, and he tried to push her away, but Keelin gripped his hip and pulled him back into her mouth.

He grew impossibly hard in her mouth. When he was right on the edge, she released him and pulled him down to her onto the quilt. "I want you inside of me when you come," she told him. "I want you to look at me."

Lucian had no issue with that. With one hard thrust, he claimed his female.

Keelin cried out beneath him, arching her back to take him more fully inside of her.

"Ye will come with me this time, lass. Ye hear me?" No matter how close he was to losing it, this would not be a repeat of their first time. Never again. "Come with me, Keelin."

He caught her wrists and held them above her head, stretching her luscious body out beneath him. Bracing himself on his elbow, he took her nipple in his mouth and nipped it with his teeth.

Her body bowed upward, and she tightened around him as her orgasm peaked.

"Keelin…" Her name was a moan against her breast.

"Lucian, please," she begged.

With a growl, he thrust into her, deep and hard. He worked his free hand between them until his thumb found her clit.

Keelin tensed and cried out again, her stomach

clenching and her sheath convulsing around him. Lucian roared, pushing deep within her as his own release came, hot and hard. It went on and on, wringing him dry, until, finally, he collapsed over her.

"I cannae get close enough tae ye, Keelin," he mumbled into her neck. "I swear ye could be beneath my own skin 'n' it would no' be enough."

Breathing hard, she twined one hand in the back of his hair and rubbed the other down his back. He was worried he was too heavy, but when he tried to lift himself off of her, she held him where he was.

Lucian dropped a kiss on the side of her throat. "Ye ken Cedric will no' let me get away with what happened."

"Yes, I know."

"I have tae be back when the moon is high in the sky tomorrow night."

"Okay."

He lifted his head to look down at her. Brushing the hair from her face, he frowned. "Ye dinna seem worried."

"I'm not."

With a moan, he rolled off of her. "Och, Keelin. Ye cannae go getting involved again! I cannae keep running around with my tail between my legs. Ye have tae let me be what I am. A full-grown male wolf!"

"Even if that means letting you die?"

"Aye! Even if tha' means letting me die."

She didn't respond, just rolled onto her side to snuggle up against his heat, and his heart swelled as his arms came around her. "I won't interfere," she told him.

Somehow he didn't believe her. "Ye have tae promise me."

"I promise," she told him sweetly.

He narrowed his eyes at her, but she wasn't intimidated. "I promise," she said again. "If you promise not to run away or do anything else rash if you start feeling… weird…around me. Because of who I am," she clarified needlessly. "Promise you'll talk to me."

He brushed his thumb over her bottom lip. "I promise," he told her.

Because he was worried the soul suckers or Duana would come back around, he borrowed another set of clothes and helped her pack up everything she needed, then they got into her car and spent the night at a hotel near Arlington.

Lucian made love to her numerous times during the night, and in between they talked and she told him about her life and he told her about his until there was no way he could feel ill at ease with her.

And, yet, he did. Though the feeling was definitely becoming less.

CHAPTER 22

Lucian held Keelin's hand as he drove them back to the apartments. She'd been unusually quiet since dinner.

He glanced at her profile. "I'll pay ye back for the meal as soon as we get there. It's hard tae carry a wallet on ye when ye dinna have any clothes on."

She rolled her eyes. "Money is the last thing I'm worried about right now."

Bringing her hand to his lips, he kissed the back of it. He knew what she was worried about. It hadn't left his mind since he'd found her again. "Keelin, if I dinnae survive this night, ye must promise me ye will stay with Cedric." He'd told her what he'd found out from Sara during the night while they lay in bed, enjoying the feel of skin on skin. For the first time in his life, Lucian was finding more peace in his human form than that of his wolf.

"Don't talk like that, Lucian."

"I must, lass. Cedric is hundreds o' years older than me. He's stronger. Has a cooler head." He smiled at this, but sobered again when she didn't share his amusement. "The odds o' my besting him are verra slim."

"You made it into the pack once before, you can do it again."

"The first time I fought my way in was against Duncan, 'n' I think he let me win. I won't be so lucky this time. No' after the way I dishonored Cedric. No' after the way I ran." His face heated, but he lifted his chin and owned the shame. "If I dinna make it in, it will be nothing less than I deserve."

"Lucian—"

"Tell me ye will stay with Cedric 'n' allow him 'n' the others tae protect ye. I will no' be able tae concentrate on the fight if I'm worried about ye."

She squeezed his hand. "I'll stay with Cedric and the pack."

He studied her face, but could see no hint of deceit. "Thank ye."

A short time later, Lucian led Keelin out into the trees behind the apartments until they reached the clearing they used for occasions such as this. The pack was all there, as was Bronaugh and Heather. After he introduced Keelin to Brock's female, he took her face in his hands and ran his eyes over her features, memorizing every freckle before he kissed her soundly on the mouth. "Remember yer promise."

"Remember yours," she told him.

"Aye," he told her, and then handed her over to the other females before he turned to face the pack.

Cedric stepped forward. "As ye all ken, I'm giving Lucian the chance tae fight his way back into the pack. This is no' a normal thing, but there is no rule against it. He brought me news last night tha' could verra well have saved our hides, 'n' it's earned him one last chance tae prove himself tae me 'n' tae ye as a pack mate."

Growls of approval met his words.

"Lucian, are ye ready?"

"Aye," he said without hesitation.

Cedric nodded. "Brock?"

Brock stepped up. "Hey, Lucian."

Lucian stared at his oldest friend. "What's going on?" he asked Cedric. "Am I no' fighting ye?"

"Och, no. Ye would never win against me, Lucian. With Brock here, ye have a wee bit more o' a chance."

"And besides," Brock told him. "You owe me this."

The male was right. He did owe him. Lucian took off his shirt. "Wolf or man?"

"Man, I think," Brock told him. "If you think you can handle it."

Lucian grinned. "Oh, aye. I can handle it."

They slapped hands, and separated again. Brock handed his shirt to Heather, and planted a kiss on her cheek.

"On my word," Cedric told them.

Lucian faced off against his best friend. Aye, this was a long time coming. Brock deserved nothing more than to beat his arse into the ground for what Lucian had done. He'd been banished because of him and his selfish needs. Lived for years as a *siubhal*, a lone wolf with no pack. Lucian couldn't imagine the loneliness of living that way.

Their entire way of life was based around pack life. Although it was a wee bit different now with all of the modern conveniences, the feeling of brotherhood was still there.

Even if some of those brothers were a huge pain in the arse.

Brock put his fists up in front of his face, and Lucian did the same.

"Ready…'n'…fight!"

Cedric stepped back out of the way as Brock threw the first punch. It landed squarely on Lucian's jaw and he felt the warm, coppery taste of his own blood. The hit took him down to one knee, but he jumped back up, arms raised to block the next punch. He got in a hit to the face and a knee to the kidney before Brock danced out of the way.

His six foot seven inch friend moved like he weighed nothing at all, bouncing on the balls of his feet as he connected time and time again with Lucian's face and ribs. He held nothing back, and it wasn't long before Lucian felt his head swim and saw spots in front of his eyes.

Once, he heard a bone crack.

Without the familiar rage burning through him, it took Lucian a minute to catch up, but as soon as the adrenaline got flowing, he gave back as good as he got, until they were both bloody and bruised and swaying on their feet.

Cedric raised his arm, signaling the end of the fight.

Lucian was confused. They were both still standing.

At his look of confusion, Cedric explained, "I can no'

have either o' ye taking too long tae recuperate. I'm going tae need ye for the fight ahead. *Both* o' ye."

Lucian was suddenly surrounded by four towering males. They slapped him on the back and the side of the head, causing stars to float before his eyes and pushing him around between them in their exuberance.

He fought them off. "Get off o' me, ye bastards!"

"Och, there's our Lucian!" Duncan said. "I was beginning tae think ye'd gone soft on us."

Lucian spit blood onto the ground. "Fuck off, Duncan. Ye pain in the arse." Then he grinned, or tried to through his swollen lips, to take some of the sting from his words. Duncan *was* a pain in the arse, but Lucian was starting to suspect he'd done it on purpose.

Cedric ruffled his hair. "Let yer lass take ye home 'n' tend yer wounds. We'll talk tomorrow about what we're going tae do about Thomas."

Lucian grabbed his wrist, but didn't shove it away. Instead, he hung onto it as he told him, "Thank ye, Cedric. I dinna deserve what ye have done for me here."

"We'll see, Lucian. We'll see." With a nod, he dismissed the others.

Lucian managed to get upstairs and into his apartment without falling and making an arse of himself, though he did let Keelin support him a wee bit. As soon as he got there, she started fluttering around, running him a bath and finding the first aid supplies, then she helped him undress and got him into the tub.

Lucian groaned as the hot water soothed his aches. But as Keelin bent over to get a towel from the linen closet, he found there was one ache the water wasn't helping at all.

He reached for her calf, but she moved out of the way before he could get a good grip on her leg.

She turned and laid the towel on the floor, then put her hands on her hips and made a face at the bloody water. "You know, I can heal you even faster than your shifter blood." Her eyes met his. "If you would let me."

Lucian felt chills shiver across his skin. "I'll just wait it out, I think." She dropped her eyes, and he quickly added, "But thank ye, lass. I do appreciate the offer."

"Well, is there *anything* I can do to help you hurt less?"

"Aye, ye can get in this bath with me." He gripped his biggest ache beneath the water, running his hand up and down the length, moaning when it did nothing at all to ease him. "I hurt, Keelin. I hurt for ye, lass."

She smiled, and pulled her shirt over her head. Her boots, socks, and jeans followed. "Let's get you washed up and out of that dirty water and I'll see what I can do."

Lucian sat up so she could wash his back, and felt a strange sense of peace descend, cloaking his soul much like the hot water did his sore body. "I love ye, Keelin. Ye ken that, dinna ye?"

"Aye," she teased. "I ken that."

* * *

Thank you for reading! I hope you loved Lucian and Keelin's story. The next book in The Kincaid Werewolves series is
A Wolf's Treasure.
Duncan's carefree charm is hiding a deeper, physical pain, one that he keeps hidden from everyone. Will Ryanne be

able to break through his defenses and prove to him he is more male than he believes?

READ A WOLF'S TREASURE NOW

" I just loved these Scottish werewolves, and Duncan can dance-
be still my heart!"
- Amazon Review

"These two together. 😍
Duncan has some trauma from the war that Ryanne triggers
memories of.
I may have shed a tear during this scene." -Goodreads review

L.E. Wilson writes Paranormal Romance starring intense alpha males and the women who are fearless enough to tame them — for the most part anyway. ;) In her novels you'll find smoking hot scenes, a touch of suspense, some humor, a bit of gore, and multifaceted characters, all working together to combine her lifelong obsession with the paranormal and her love of romance.

Her writing career came about the usual way: on a dare from her loving husband. Little did she know just one casual suggestion would open a box of worms (or words as the case may be) that would forever change her life.

Peach tea and her tiara are a necessary part of her writing process, though sometimes you'll find her typing away at her favorite Starbucks. She walks two miles to get there, to make up for all of those coffees. On the weekends she likes to hike, garden, cook vegan food, and have date nights with her favorite guy.

On a Personal Note:
"I love to hear from my readers! Contact me anytime at le@lewilsonauthor.com."

Keep In Touch With L.E.
lewilsonauthor.com
le@lewilsonauthor.com